BEST

GAY

EROTICA

2008

BEST
GAY
EROTICA
2008

Series Editor

RICHARD LABONTÉ

Selected and Introduced by

EMANUEL XAVIER

CLEIS
PRESS

Published in the United States.
Cleis Press Inc., P.O. Box 14697, San Francisco, California 94114

Printed in the United States.
Cover design: Scott Idleman
Cover photograph: Celesta Danger
Text design: Frank Wiedemann
Cleis logo art: Juana Alicia
First Edition.
10 9 8 7 6 5 4 3 2 1

Always for Asa

CONTENTS

FOREWORD

For all the hundreds and hundreds of erotic short stories published each year, in other collections, in magazines, and online, not a lot of cream—or spunk—rises to the top. One of my favorite science fiction writers, Theodore Sturgeon, is said to have said, crankily, that ninety-nine percent of everything is crap. True enough. Every year, I aim, along with the guest judge, to find that other one percent—to lap up whatever rises to, or spills over, the top.

Regular readers of *Best Gay Erotica* will recognize a few familiar names in this year's edition: Simon Sheppard (absent from just one of the *BGE*s), Wayne Courtois, Shane Allison, Jeff Mann, Alana Noël Voth, horehound stillpoint, and Andy Quan, all of whom have made one or more appearances over the thirteen years of this series. Some are new to the book, though they've been published elsewhere: Taylor Siluwé, Sam J. Miller, Tim Miller, Jason Shults, and Tom Cardamone. Different voices, different styles, different kinks, with quality as the common denominator.

But it's a particular pleasure to include first-time writers—new to publication, or at least new to me. There are five such authors this year, more than usual: Lee Houck, mixing sexual memories with the immediacy of an encounter out of control; Arden Hill, writing about the power of cool seduction; Charlie Vazquez, with a story about the rewards of role reversal in sex play; Rhidian Brenig Jones, whose tale explores how good sex is a salve that eases the pain of love gone wrong; and Andrew McCarthy, whose characters exult in the thrill of public sex.

It's fitting that there are more novices than usual this year: Emanuel Xavier, who selected the "bests" for 2008, had his own publishing debut in *Best Gay Erotica 1997* with the short story "Motherfuckers," an excerpt from what became the novel *Christ-Like*. It's been more than a decade since we met; in that time, he rose to poetry slam prominence, curated a trendsetting reading series at A Different Light Bookstore in New York in the 1990s, founded the glamorous House of Xavier (fusing the excitement of the ballroom scene with the energy of the spoken word movement), published the poetry collections *Pier Queen* and *Americano*, and edited the spoken-word collection *Bullets & Butterflies*. It's been a treat to spend time with him again, crafting this latest edition of *Best Gay Erotica*.

Richard Labonté
Calabogie, Ontario / Bowen Island, British Columbia
August 2007

INTRODUCTION: FINDING MYSELF IN THE NARRATIVE

Emanuel Xavier

It's easy to forget we are a nation at war when sex is everywhere around us—the front pages of newspapers, all over the Internet, used to sell everything from cars to shoes to kitchen appliances. Gay sex is fashionable and mainstream. Even if it's subtle, all one has to do is pick up a magazine or turn on the television. I would be a hypocrite to claim not to indulge in such pleasures because I would rather focus on the realities of the world. Let's face it—if every consenting adult could enjoy sex without repercussions, the world would be a better place.

Previous judges for *Best Gay Erotica* have often complained how hard it is to choose which erotic short stories make the final cut. I found it's not really that difficult. Stories forwarded to me from editor Richard Labonté either left me hot and bothered or had me curling into bed with my cats. The submissions I truly enjoyed made me close my eyes and jerk off until I stained them. Lube and cum stains sealed the selection of each finalist found in this collection.

Yeah, *papi*, they were that good!

Bests are good: after all, who wants to get really drunk, shut off the lights and go to bed with an "It'll do for the night!" collection? Short stories should also hold up to sobriety and proper lighting in the morning. I have always wanted to be a total slut, to receive a diverse selection of erotic short stories, and to be asked to decide which work as both erotica and art. I knew deep inside I would get great submissions demonstrating the talents of creative individuals.

I must admit this collection should be titled *Best Gay Erotica 2008 According to a Latino Former Prostitute Turned Poet.* No one can truly claim these are the "best" gay erotic short stories of the year—but they're certainly the best from among the several hundred submitted to Richard. I know for a fact he suffered through hours and hours of crap that wouldn't get even a scat fetishist off. So I make no apologies for getting turned on by the stories featured in this collection. I'll keep it real: as with slam poetry, there is a lot of competition in writing erotica. Submitting your work to any publication is a quiet contest—much like walking around in a towel at a sex club, hoping to get laid by hot guys before your time is up, and so desperate you're willing to have sex with a troll. But I digress.

The word *best* is not quite as problematic as the word *erotica*. With so much hard-core sex and pornography thrown at us, *erotica* is a challenging word to define. It's "works of art, including literature, photography, film, sculpture and painting, which deal substantively with erotically stimulating or arousing descriptions." Or it's "a modern word used to describe the portrayal of the human anatomy and sexuality with high-art aspirations, differentiating such work from commercial pornography." However, artists are forever pushing boundaries in their attempts to be provocative; at another extreme, "erotica" has been violently abused, left behind in some cheap hotel with a used condom sticking out of its ass. I'm happy to say that, while there are condoms in some of the stories here, there's also a lot of art.

After Richard sifted through the submitted works of art, I received a stack of his favorites, with the author's names deleted. It was truly awesome to discover, after the fact, that I was not familiar with more than half of the finalists. My picks had nothing to do with the writers' reputations within the genre: I based my choices on the quality of the anonymous writing... and weighed the impact of the stories against my own active and healthy sex life. At times, I found myself trying to figure out if I knew the author, had ever had sex with him, or even wanted to collaborate for mutual stimulation. As any narcissistic reader would, I imagined myself one of the characters in each story. But without knowing the authors' identities until after I had made my selections, I was able to enjoy each submission not because I was physically (or intellectually) attracted to the writer, but because I found myself in each of these narratives.

As a writer, I read for inspiration, with the hope that emotions I never knew existed will be provoked. The erotica here offers a wide-ranging public glimpse into the private sexual desires of each of the authors—but it's all consensual, and it's all inviting. With so much going on in my world, I read mostly for simple pleasure. I got that, and so much more, from this collection.

My very first publication was a short story titled "Mother-fuckers" in *Best Gay Erotica 1997* (also featured later in *Best of Best Gay Erotica*). Even then, I knew to stay away from using certain words, the kind that elicited fits of laughter in the bedroom. For example, "mangina" would get any story trying to date me directions to the nearest exit. As a pet lover and a survivor of sexual abuse, I shunned any stories that involved harming pets or children. Likewise, as a person of color, any stories obsessed with white supremacy were snubbed. On the other hand, the subtle introduction of a condom was a definite plus. Some of the submissions seemed as if their authors were more interested in shocking than actually inviting the reader into their private worlds and arousing anything other than awe. Maybe I'm jaded, but an erotic story should excite the reader with its imagination, besides providing pleasure.

The tales I ultimately selected widened my eyes with the recognition of real people seeking to unwind from their everyday lives by sexually connecting to others. These were erotic adventures that took me on a thrilling journey, sometimes dropping me off when it was over in the familiar front of my apartment, other times leaving me somewhere out on a strange and exciting open road. The voices featured in *Best Gay Erotica 2008* eroticized real experiences and, sometimes playfully, sometimes surprisingly, revealed genuine desire.

As I read, I wondered how self-aware the writers were about having the reader indulge in their fantasies; I often sensed a smile on their mischievous faces as they challenged our own sexual constraints. Andrew McCarthy's "Underground Operator," Wayne Courtois' "Capturing the King," and dirty daddy horehound stillpoint's "Donuts to Demons" are perfect examples of such stories.

Among these selected short stories, there is both pain and joy. A story by Lee Houck delves deeply into bondage, Simon Sheppard's dabbles in hustling, Shane Allison's poetic confessions draw deeply on his memories and Alana Noël Voth's "Release" is all about longing; there is a Tim Miller performance classic, plenty of twosomes and threesomes, and a piss party as imagined by Charlie Vazquez. More improvised fantasies or off-the-cuff cravings motivate Arden Hill's "My Boy Tuesday," Jeff Mann's "Snowed in with Sam," Jason Shults' "Minimum Damage, Minimum Pain," and the fantasies of the gay couple in Sam J. Miller's "Short Sad Sordid Sexual Encounters." Whether the characters featured are simply exploring their passions, as in Taylor Siluwé's "Breeding Season," or getting over relationships, as in Rhidian Brenig Jones' "Come to Light," it can be said that the root of all good erotica is love. Even the most provocative erotica, if carefully read, reveals the need to connect on a deeper level. Sometimes through these stories we discover things that arouse us about which we may not have been fully aware. Whatever emotional demands a short story such as Tom Cardamone's "Funeral Clothes" or Andy Quan's "The Best Sex between Them" places on us, at least we are able to relate to the writers and enjoy the ride. The result is a celebration of the pleasures of gay sex.

So welcome to a diversity of voices, revel in an exploration of sexuality and a range of desires and indulge yourselves with the anthology—and remember, the authors are not always their characters. Erotica writers are often not what we imagine them to be, which says a lot about all of us on a more intimate level.

Finally, thanks to Cleis Press for trusting me with this collection, and to Richard, whose first book as editor was the *Best Gay Erotica* in which I made my debut, for making the selection process so easy. And thanks, of course, to the seventeen writers featured, for providing me (and now all of you) with such splendid pleasure.

Brooklyn, New York
August 2007

MY BOY TUESDAY

Arden Hill

He needed a name so I named him Tuesday.
Tuesday for the day we met in Professor Alice Adams' section of Shakespeare's Women.
I was wearing my hair blond and blue then,
so of course he noticed me when he walked
in the door, though I have no doubt he would
have, even if I'd tried to blend in. Blending in
is one of the few things I don't excel at. It is an
art I choose not to explore. Tuesday was wearing worn brown pants, both knees reinforced
with bright green patches. They said to me,
"Hello, I kneel down a lot," and so I smiled at
them before following the slouchy lines of his
body up to a subdued green sweater, solid not
striped, soft and patchless. He had a sweet face
and when I looked down at my watch I noted
he was three minutes late for class. I fantasized

about punishing him for this, slapping him hard. And when he became hard enough, I would tie his right hand to his ankles and tell him to make himself come for me with his left one. I would reward him for this act.

When Tuesday came to class that first day, he tucked his backpack quietly under the chair in front of him, a chair only feet away from mine, so I could see the small pink triangle he'd pinned to the bag's zipper, and the red ribbon that was tied around the zipper. I remember licking my lips and smiling. It's always easier when they know they're gay. I've spent too many semesters with football players sucking my cock, their massive shoulder muscles heaving as they weep salt tears over my come and their spit. When they can breathe again they always say the same thing. "Tristan, man, I think I might be gay. I really liked that. I really liked sucking you off." If I'm not in a bad mood I tell them it was okay, but if I'm pissy, and I mean pissy about anything that happened that day—lousy parking, a dull class, a cold cup of coffee—I tell them, "Well you might be gay now, you big faggot, but that blow job just turned me straight." Those big boys don't wear my collar. They call me by my name. I don't officially top them but it's always there to some degree, and it was there even in the beginning when I was the one down on the floor. When I'm mean to lovers that aren't bottoms they leave and don't come back. Fine. If I'm mean to Tuesday, he might cry a little but I'm sure he'd roll over and stick his ass up in the air for me to cane, or fuck, or just stare at until he wiggles and moans and I decide to be nice.

I can relate to boys like Tuesday, or rather I can remember what it was like to assume that position. I was nineteen. My lover was twenty-six. "Hey boy," he said, "I want to teach you something." He pushed my arms out past my head and jerked back on my ankles until they were next to his knees. The lube was cold when he stuck his finger into my ass but by the time he worked his dick in it was warm, almost burning. "Oh you like that you little slut," he said and he reached for his belt, the one I'd taken off with my teeth earlier in the evening. He hit me twenty-five times across each shoulder. I imagined his hand holding the belt. No. I imagined my hand on the leather. When he had me count out loud I heard the numbers as though it were his voice speaking and I smiled between each word. He told me thank him and I did, though he had no idea what I was thanking him for.

The next night he learned what I'd gathered from his lesson. He said I could tie him up if I wanted. I did, and I did it with the cuffs and joiners he'd used on me earlier. I whipped him lightly and he moaned, his mouth falling open with each flick of leather across his skin. I tightened the restraints and he looked up at me with surprise but delight. I put on a glove and pushed two fingers into him. His dick rose up. I could almost hear it humming. "Oh you like that you little slut," I growled. He gave me a cocky sort of smile before I shoved the gag in his mouth. I put in more fingers and he rocked on my hand. "Now that you're in a position to listen," I said, "our relationship is going to be different and if you're not up for that difference our relationship is going to be over." I undid the gag so he could whisper, "Yes Sir."

I put the gag back in and told him that I'd been thinking about what I did and did not like in bed. I told him he was not going to be allowed to touch my cock. Well, not with his hands at least. Before this moment I endured the feel of my silk underpants shifting to sandpaper as clumsy hands rubbed me through denim. Once my pants were off, too many lovers groped me, tugging and pulling until I was hard but hurting. I put up with it because I liked what happened next, when they thought they had warmed me up enough to lick my dick lightly with the tips of their tongues. I like to be taken on the tongue like a thick wafer, one that does not dissolve but still induces someone to murmur Jesus. I like to spill down a throat. I slipped out the gag and thrust into him, showing him. He swallowed and when I pulled out he thanked me. I realized then other things I liked: downcast eyes, the strands of hair that fall across the forehead after someone has exerted himself.

Tuesday had run down the hallway in an attempt to make it to class on time. His black bangs were wet. There was a damp curl twisting down the collar of his shirt. I watched him and took notes on Shakespeare's women and my own soon-to-be boy both. I could imagine him on his knees while I, dressed in a gown, lifted up layer after layer of fabric until there was nothing between my cock and his mouth but silk. I would bind his hands first. I would write what I liked on notes that I would not let him read until class. I would have him sit in a different spot, to my left and ahead just a bit so I could watch him read but it would still be clear we were not equals, not in the bedroom, not in any room.

The professor asked a question and Tuesday's slim hand shot up. *Eager*, I remarked to myself, and when Tuesday spoke I liked the tones of his answer. His voice cracked a little on the name Titania, and I knew I wanted him to wear glitter and answer my questions, ending each sentence with a slight and cracking "Sir." The professor looked pleased, which indicated to me that Tuesday is a good reader. I am a good writer. I know this is going to work out. He shifted in his chair a bit and turned around as though my gaze had weight. He looked at me then looked down. He knew from the beginning where this was going. Tuesday was a very bright boy.

After class Tuesday wandered over to my desk. Although articulate with literature, he seemed shy about practical matters, so I told him to come over to my apartment on Wednesday. I took his hand and wrote my address on the back of it. I did not ask for his address. We did not exchange names or numbers. I was certain he'd show up and if he didn't, well I knew where to find him, and I've noticed other boys in this class who I could entice over, boys whose bruises would make Tuesday sorry he did not accept what I offered. I am not stingy, but careful, with my kindnesses.

Tuesday put on his backpack and promised to arrive at my place on time. I wrote *seven* on his wrist. Black ink over the blue of his veins. He smiled, and since I am careful with my compliments I did not tell him that his mouth is perfect. As he walked out I noticed that his ass matches it beautifully. I'd like to fill his ass and his mouth at the same time. I have the evening to decide what will go in each hole. I briefly wonder if Tuesday has a preference and suspect that I will learn. What I will do with that knowledge, I haven't decided. I imagine him grateful. I imagine him suffering. In both circumstances, Tuesday's cheeks are wet with tears and his naked chest is crossed with claw marks.

I like my nails long. Sometimes I paint them with slightly black-tinged gloss so that they shine like talons. Once, when I was at the counter of the grocery store preparing to pay for a package of strawberries, the scruffy man looked at my hands and not my face. He said, "That will be three dollars, Miss." Slightly amused, I responded, "Here you go," as I handed him the bills. "Oh," he gasped looking up, "I thought you were a woman." I pulled the berries from his hands and hissed, "If you were paying attention you would have realized I'm a goddess." I strode out before he could respond.

Everyone has his kink. Mine has a feminine bent. "Don't even think of calling me anything other than Sir," I tell the boys as I take off my panties. Anyone who looks skeptical earns an hour in my drag closet with the instruction not to come out until he is beautiful. Then I take him out for a night on the town. I put on the corresponding clothes, a three-piece suit with my father's favorite tie. We look like a het couple so I buy the girl/boy dinner. I have her/him eat out my ass for dessert.

I think about Tuesday while I am making myself dinner. I am hungry and hungry makes me horny. Something about satiation causes the wires in my brain to cross so that after I fuck a boy, after I come inside him emptying a cock full of cream into his body, I myself feel full. I no longer crave anything but, perhaps, to watch the boy clean himself off with a warm wet rag. With the jocks I've fucked there is no ritual. I send them home immediately after and I do not care how they brush their teeth or scrub their asses raw in the shower. I've been called a bitch on more than one occasion. "Frigid bitch," was the phrase used by the last quarterback after he told me that he loved me and I told him that I wasn't interested in fucking him anymore. He called me frigid and I watched my come cool on his chest.

My thoughts about Tuesday are more tender. I make three portions of tomato sauce, one for me to eat tonight and the other two for us to share on Wednesday. I want him to watch me eat and feel hungry before it is his turn. I want to hand-feed this one. I want to play sweet master, for a while. A mediocre top once told me, "You can't top someone if you're serving them food." I liked neither his phrasing nor his twitchy eyes. I assured him it could be done and pointed out that he didn't deserve for me to prove it to him. Instead, I invited his favorite submissive play partner over and tied him up in my shower. I washed him outside and in. He wept when the water ran cold. I commanded him not to tremble while I patted him dry so gently that he ached to press his hard cock into the towel and hump it until he came but I never let him come. I dressed him up and set him at the dinner table. With one hand, I grasped his throat. With the other, I fed him small bites of vegetable lasagna. I chewed each bite first and, when he looked thirsty, I put water in my mouth and spat it into his. He didn't play with that top again, a decision I'm sure was influenced by his encounter with me. Everyone has his kink and I have a talent for turning people on to mine.

I don't think about Tuesday again until I am bathing. I've poured in a small amount of bubble bath and the white sides of the tub are as smooth and slick as I imagine the head of his cock will be. The water gradually warms the enamel and I push my back down against the bottom. My cock swells and breaks the surface of the water. It bursts bubbles and I fixate on Tuesday's ass, how I want to ease in while he pants at the difficulty of having me there. I haven't seen him around, which means that he is a freshman and, although he has a pink triangle on his bag, the button is new enough that it may have just been put on. He is pretty, but then so are boy bands. I suppose it would not have been difficult for him to be read as straight in high school. Even if people suspected he was gay, he is the kind of pretty that rivals a girl's good looks. Most guys are too scared to ask a boy like that out on a date much less get their dicks into him.

While it is highly likely that young Tuesday is a virgin, I find it impossible to believe that he hasn't stuck anything up his own ass. I decide that I will make him catalogue those objects between bites of dinner. Eventually I will put the spider gag on him. I want to enjoy the sight of his mouth open. Maybe the second time he comes over I will start there and work my way down. For our first time, I am exclusively interested in his ass.

I sleep well after my bath. I dream about an old building with many rooms. It looks unmistakably like my college though instead of classrooms there are cells. I walk down the halls and hear the sounds of boys fucking. The doors are oak and each has a window that is placed exactly at my eye level. I look into the first door that I come to and see Tuesday inside, hog-tied on top of Professor Alice Adams' desk. The room is populated by the men's lacrosse team. They stare at Tuesday because he is naked and beautiful. They want him but they are only students who will, at most, witness the lesson. A door next to the chalkboard opens and Alice Adams walks in. No, she struts in. She struts toward her desk in a black latex suit that forms the curves of her body into straight lines. A huge pink strap-on protrudes from her fly and Tuesday's eyes widen as she pulls a condom out of a mysterious and previously unnoticed back pocket. Alice Adams walks past the desk and Tuesday follows her with his eyes. They are the only parts of his body that can move and he stares as Alice Adams hands the condom to a redheaded boy in the front row. The boy blushes brighter than his freckles as she orders him to put his hands behind his back and put the condom on her cock using only his mouth. Once he completes the task to her satisfaction, she rewards him with a piece of chocolate to take away the taste of latex on his tongue.

Alice Adams' cock is wet with this boy's spit when she shoves it between Tuesday's lips. He grunts and gulps until he deep-throats her. The door I am peeping through opens and I find my cock in my hand ready to fuck. I spread Tuesday's ass and spit on the trembling red opening that reveals itself to me. Alice Adams and I fuck him until the three of us come, me first, Alice second, and Tuesday third. I wake up gripping the sheets. There are hours to fill until my doorbell rings.

I get some work done on my thesis: The Erotics of the Sonnet. I've been working on this project all summer and although it is only the first week of classes, I can think of no bigger turnoff than a fourteen-line poem. Maybe a haiku formed from a magnetic poetry set. The only set I've ever appreciated was the set of "dirty" magnetic poetry that I got from my dyke cousin Jodie. There are no less than ten rectangles that read *cock*. The adjectives are impressive, from the functional, *hard*, to the more metaphorical, *effervescent*. I would like to have Tuesday compose poems with the set while sitting on a sterling silver butt plug. He'd look darling in just a white button-down shirt and a tie. He'd be pantless so I could see the plug penetrate him and run my fingers along the crevice between perineum and metal when I wanted to distract him from his task. I know this would be unfair of me but I am not attempting to be fair. I would rather dish out what a bottom needs than indulge him in what he thinks he wants. I am insidiously benevolent. My gifts are gifts. My punishments are also gifts, when viewed with the right interpretation. This is not Orwellian doublespeak, but a truth I'm sure a bright boy like Tuesday will be able to grasp.

In my house, the pleasures of the bedroom extend beyond its walls, so in preparation for Tuesday's arrival, I clean every room. I like the possibility of taking him anyplace. Every space in the house is ready. The tables and counters are clear. The floors are clean enough to eat off of. I pull a large wooden box out from under my bed and lay the gear out on a towel. I unwrap each cock, each plug, each chain, each strap, and each clip. I polish the leather with saddle soap, shine the steel, and wipe down the rest with alcohol swabs and a hint of lavender. I put everything away but a blindfold before the doorbell rings. Wanting has grown in me like a horse pounding its hooves, steam rolling out of its nostrils like the blackest aspect of fire. I conjure spurs and a whip. I tighten myself till I am calm, then I open the door and lead Tuesday in. He trembles as he kneels before me and I brush his black bangs aside to tie the blindfold. His breath is measured and I feel him sinking into where I want him, but before he goes down too deeply, I give him his safeword. I inhale. I begin.

CAPTURING THE KING

Wayne Courtois

The vast acreage of the Thorne estate was far removed from town. None of the family was left now except for old Mrs. Thorne, attended by nurses who were constantly coming and going from the main house. And no one else lived on the estate anymore—no one but Brian and Powell.

Brian worked in the greenhouse, maintaining the orchids. It had been old man Thorne's wish that, upon his death, the exotic plants would be cared for in perpetuity. So Brian had a guaranteed job for life, and free lodgings in what was once the gardener's cottage. In a way it was a strange prospect for a young man, that he might be living and working in this remote spot for—what, the next forty years? On the surface, it didn't seem like much. But the cottage more than suited his needs; he had even turned one of its rooms into a weight room, with the latest bodybuilding equipment. His trips to town kept him in books and music, and an occasional man to spend the night with. As comfortable as he was, he had no need to think about moving on.

And then there was Powell.

Powell—first name? Last name? Brian didn't know—was also a young man who had been employed on the estate for a few years, beginning as a chauffeur. But those few short years had brought a lot of change, beginning with the death of old Mr. Thorne and the declining health of his widow. Since a chauffeur was hardly needed anymore, Powell took on other responsibilities as the older staff moved on or retired. Now he was even handling the estate's financial matters.

And Powell was, as far as Brian was concerned, a King. A Nubian King.

Sometimes Brian would look at Powell from afar—their daily lives didn't intersect very much, they even ate their meals at different times—and suddenly realize that he was standing and staring with his mouth open. Where did he *come* from, this man with the noble bearing and beautiful dark skin? Oh, Brian had been looking at men for a long time, as long as he could remember; but he'd never seen a man who *moved* like that...his graceful assertiveness was poetry for the eyes. There was Powell, in the black outfit from his chauffeur days, striding down the great lawn to talk to the yard workers who came out from town twice a month. Some of these guys were sexy, yes, and weren't shy about taking their shirts off as they worked. But they were nothing compared to Powell.

Once, when Brian and Powell had happened to be in the main house at the same time, Brian had struck up a conversation, none-too-subtly mentioning that the orchid got its name from a Greek word meaning "testes," because of the way the bulbs looked. "If you come down to the greenhouse sometime, you can see mine," he said. "My plants, I mean!" Even as he felt his face turning red he kept his eyes on Powell, who seemed to give him a fleeting look—a meaningful one. *God,* Brian thought, *what am I doing*? Another time Brian, crossing the grounds on his way to the greenhouse, spotted Powell outside the garage that housed Mrs. Thorne's Mercedes. The car was of no use to her anymore, but Powell kept it in good condition. Today he was washing the car in the driveway...and he was...*naked.*

Well, almost naked. He wore black swim trunks—not a Speedo but close to it. And why not, it was a hot day, the hottest day of summer so far. Ducking behind a tree, Brian found he could get a good view of the young man without, hopefully, being seen. Except for his swim trunks and sunglasses, Powell *was* naked, and he'd perspired enough that his muscular frame gleamed in the sun.

If only I could see the soles of his feet! Brian thought. *Then I could die happy.*

He watched Powell all through the washing, rinsing, and waxing of the car. In an almost unbearable state of arousal, Brian brushed his hand against his crotch and realized that he had come in his shorts, without knowing just when.

His chore done, Powell walked away. Brian could swear that the barely-glimpsed soles of those feet were winking at him.

One night not long after that, Brian, who had his own car, drove to the nearest gay bar, thirty miles away. It was the kind of place—pool table, dance floor the size of a hand towel—that always seemed larger in memory than it did in reality. But it attracted guys from many miles around, including some just passing through, so Brian usually saw at least a few new faces, all the more so since he rarely dropped by. He was used to the looks he got as soon as he entered—*Hey, check it out, this guy is hot*—and he absorbed them without, he hoped, seeming arrogant as he made his way to the bar while avoiding eye contact with anyone. He needed at least one beer to overcome his shyness.

He'd barely taken a sip when a guy appeared at his elbow, ordering a beer but also cutting his eyes toward Brian, desperate to put the moves on him. After about thirty seconds Brian returned a glance, enough to get the picture. Not a bad-looking guy—shorter than Brian, shaved head, dark coating of stubble on his face, slim but well built. Brown eyes that were lively, mischievous. His name was Scott, and during some small talk Brian found out what he needed to know, taking a light, playful poke at Scott's ribs. Scott jumped.

"Ticklish?" Brian asked. Just saying the word *ticklish* brought a flush to his face, and his dick stiffened a bit.

"*Very* ticklish," Scott said, almost proudly, as if it showed just how much fun he could be.

He had no idea.

Even the headlights of Scott's Jeep seemed eager, bouncing in Brian's rearview mirror as they followed the rough country roads back to the estate. When they pulled into the cottage drive, Scott was the first one out of his car. "Wow," he said, "you were right, this place really is isolated."

"Lots of privacy," Brian said, fitting his key in the lock.

"Great!"

As soon as he was inside, Scott stripped off his T-shirt. Oh, *very* nice build. Hairy chest, and a treasure trail leading from his navel to the waist of his jeans, which didn't stay on for long. Nor did Brian take long to get to the matter at hand; he couldn't, he was too excited. As they kissed, greedy with their tongues, Brian's fingers took nips here and there, at Scott's rib cage, his sides, up into his armpits. Scott gasped and wriggled, pulled his mouth away from Brian's long enough to say, "I told you I was ticklish."

That was the last thing Scott would say for a while, because Brian wasn't about to stop. His hands moved swiftly, attacking Scott's sides, belly, ribs and armpits. Scott tried to defend himself, but he was always one step behind Brian's probing, poking, squeezing fingers. It was easy to steer Scott into the bedroom, where the ticklish young man, nearly hysterical, collapsed onto the bed. Brian was right on top of him. Having mapped Scott's most tender spots—lower ribs, armpits, sides—he kept at them, his victim's high-pitched laughter and squeals of protest egging him on. Straddling his hips, Brian admired the view: Scott's hairy, helpless torso, big hard dick riding up on his belly…. Scott was still struggling too much for the tickling to be most effective, but Brian knew the cure for that: *more tickling.* "Oh yeah," he said, "I'm gonna keep tickling you, stud, so get used to it. The more you struggle, the sooner you'll be too exhausted to fight me off. Then we'll *really* have some fun. You haven't felt *anything* yet!"

Scott's eyes rolled in panic; his fingers clawed helplessly at the air as Brian kept him pinned down. Ribs, armpits, sides… back and forth, back and forth. Plus there were two sweet spots just above his hips…when Brian squeezed there, Scott's laughter turned to desperate, hoarse panting. His struggling body weakened, he sagged back onto the mattress as the tension left him…even as that was happening, Brian knew, Scott was terrified that his body was succumbing to this torture, and soon wouldn't be able to struggle at all. "That's just what I'm waiting for, baby," Brian said. "Waiting till you're weak and helpless and can't move at all."

When the time came, Brian left Scott lying there, the poor man's chest heaving, limbs too weak to move on the sweat-soaked sheet. In his dresser Brian found his soft restraints—they were made from old bathrobe belts—and began to tie Scott's wrists and ankles to the bedposts as the young man stared with anguish and fear in his eyes. When he felt the cloth being fastened around his ankle, he managed to struggle a bit.

"What's that, baby?" Brian asked. "Are you telling me your feet are ticklish?"

More struggling, though it was so ineffective that it was embarrassing—and wonderful—to watch. Brian finished tying off the young man's wrists and ankles. Scott was squirming, pulling on his bonds, finding that he was indeed trapped and helpless. His cock was harder than ever. He tried to speak, but could barely do more than whisper. Brian obligingly brought his ear close to Scott's lips.

"Please...please let me go."

Brian stood up, patted Scott's shaved head. "I like that, hearing you beg. You'll be doing a lot more begging before I'm through, I promise you that."

Over the next hour or so Brian devoted himself to finding out just how ticklish Scott's shapely, size-10 feet were. Their responsiveness was never less than amazing. After bringing Scott to a series of hoarse, nearly silent screams, Brian said, "Oh shit, this is too good, I have to bring everything out now." Returning to his dresser, he found the cloth bag that held his collection. Feathers, some soft, some stiff. A hairbrush with long, mean-looking bristles. An old toothbrush, a plastic fork.... He showed each of these things to Scott, telling him that they would be used on his feet, even though it might take several hours to go through them all. Scott looked like he could faint, or wanted to.

"Don't worry," Brian said, "I won't hurt you. I'm just going to tickle you, that's all. Here, let me get you some water."

After Scott had his drink he was able to speak a bit. "Please... don't t-tickle me anymore...."

Brian shook his head. "Oh, you poor baby," he said. "Do you know how it makes my dick *ache* to hear you say that?"

Brian was good to his word, using every tool in his kit on poor Scott's feet. By the time a couple of hours had passed, Scott was in another world entirely, a world of nothing but tickle torture, and whenever it seemed as bad as it could get, there was another level to break through. It was a world of unthinkable torment, outrageous suffering, where a minute could seem like an hour; in that hour he could be tickled to death a thousand times, only to keep reviving to a world of blinding agony. His voice long since destroyed by screaming, all he could do was pant as his torturer found fresh delights in his sexy, helpless skin. Brian was using feathers now, for Scott had been sensitized to the *n*th degree, and the merest touch of a frond turned his face into a mask of pleading: *Oh for god's sake, kill me, kill me now...just don't* tickle *me anymore!*

Brian came many times during the night, often without touching himself. The feel of Scott's ribs under his fingertips, or the sight of his soft soles with the bristles of a brush pressed against them, was enough to give him a spontaneous orgasm. He made sure that Scott had several mind-blowing climaxes also. A lot of the cum landed on his body, which made things more interesting. The hot, sticky cream had to be removed if it was covering a ticklish spot, and Brian's technique with tongue or washcloth was its own kind of torture. It was heaven to watch Scott's panicked expression and listen to his whispered screams as Brian reamed out his navel with rough terrycloth. "That's right, baby," he said. "Your ticklish nerve-ends are mine, all mine."

Sometime toward morning, Brian woke to find himself lying with his toes jammed into Scott's armpits, his fingers stroking Scott's feet. If he didn't know better, he'd think that he had been tickling Scott while he dozed. Maybe he had! Scott was certainly out of it. *Oh, Jesus,* Brian thought, *there's nothing more fun than a super-ticklish guy who's been tickled all night!* He stepped up his lazy stroking of those soles until Scott began to squirm again. Yeah, this was the best: a totally delirious victim with his wagging tongue and sloppy, involuntary grins…. Scott looked at Brian with eyes that didn't seem to be able to focus, and when he tried to speak, all that came out was gibberish.

"I'm enjoying this too much, buddy," Brian said. "I'm gonna have to tickle you for a couple more hours, at least." Crawling toward the head of the bed, he sank into his victim, caressing his abs, tickling the piss out of him. Luxuriating in the madness of it, and the smell of beer-piss, panic sweat, and cum.

At last, sometime after sunrise, he untied the restraints. Scott didn't move. "I've just about tickled you to death, haven't I?" Brian asked. He brought a glass of water, but Scott was too weak to hold it. Brian sat on the edge of the bed for a while as the young man gradually came back to life, such as it was: exhausted, overstimulated, his flesh mottled as if he were blushing all over. It took several tries before he could move his legs over the side of the bed and sit up. He sat there for a while, now and then raising a fingertip to touch himself here and there—testing a rib or much-abused armpit, letting go a soft hysterical giggle.

"Try to stand up," Brian said.

Scott looked at Brian as if he were seeing him for the first time. He had been so immersed in a world of sensation that the real world was registering slowly; he was still getting used to the idea that he wasn't tied down anymore. He rubbed one wrist, then the other. Looked down at his poor roughed-up feet on the carpet. Surely he remembered, amid all the unbearable tickling, how his cock had burst like a firecracker time after time? When he regarded his torturer now, it was with fear and desire mixed. But fear won out. Moving stiffly, he fumbled for his jeans and managed to get them on. Grabbed his shirt in one hand, his sneakers and socks in the other, and walked a drunkard's path to the door.

"Wait," Brian said. "Put your sneakers on first.... Scott, put your sneakers on!"

Too late. Once he was moving, Scott wasn't about to stop, even if he did have to walk barefoot across the gravel drive to his car. The gravel bit his tenderized soles, making him yelp each step of the way. When he finally made it to his Jeep he took off in an arc that sprayed a good bit of that gravel onto the lawn. As Brian watched the Jeep's erratic spin down the drive, he realized that Scott would probably talk. Yes: at the risk of embarrassing himself, he would warn other guys away from Brian and his particular kink.

Maybe that would be for the best. Maybe anything that gave him that much pleasure was bad. Brian couldn't believe that for long, though. He had a computer with a high-speed

Internet connection on his bedroom desk, and many nights he sat up late, looking at pictures and video clips of men bound and tickled. The barrage of unspeakably erotic images brought him to explosive orgasms as he jacked off with one hand and tickled his balls with the other. Each explosion seemed to engage all the nerve and muscle he had, and he'd sit there afterward, feeling totally drained, his vision blurred. Jesus, did everybody have orgasms like this?

Not far from the greenhouse, at the west end of the Thorne mansion, was a screened porch where Brian often ate his lunch. It was comfortable, cool and quiet. He never saw a soul as he sat facing the side lawn and the path that led to his cottage. One day, when he had finished his sandwich and thermos of iced tea, he sat back in his soft vinyl chair, put his feet up on the ottoman, and closed his eyes, telling himself he was only going to rest for a minute.

A noise from the doorway jolted him and he sat up, not knowing at first where he was. Blinking, he thought he saw Powell standing there. He shook his head and looked again. Yes, it was Powell in the doorway, holding a plate covered with a napkin.

"Mind if I come in?" he asked.

For a moment Brian could only stare. It had been so long since he'd heard Powell speak, or even seen him this close. The young man was dressed plainly, in khaki shorts like Brian's and a light blue T-shirt, flip-flops on his large feet. Once he glimpsed those feet, Brian found it almost impossible to take his eyes from them. "Oh," he said, collecting himself with great effort, "no, I don't mind. Please come in."

Powell sat in an armchair across from Brian's. He pulled

the napkin from his plate to reveal a sandwich, lettuce and tomato peeking out between thick crusts. Powell picked the whole thing up in one hand and took a bite, looking frankly at Brian as he chewed.

Brian was at a loss. Having finished his lunch, he had nothing to do with his hands, which started to tremble whenever he dared glance at Powell's feet in their flip-flops. The dark brown skin lightened between the toes and down toward the soles, as if nature had found a way to highlight the most ticklish spots. Blushing, Brian looked up to catch Powell surreptitiously licking a spot of mayo from his thumb. That tip of tongue poking through shapely lips—holy fuck! He should have gotten up and run, but all he could do was sit helplessly as Powell, his tone so smooth and relaxed, asked if everything was all right down at the cottage.

"Wh-what?" Brian asked, sounding like an idiot to himself.

"I was asking you if everything was all right down at the cottage. I saw a light down there, quite late, a few nights ago."

Brian tried to speak, but all that came out was a panicked, strangling sound. He cleared his throat and said, "I didn't know you could see that far from here."

Powell's fingertip grazed the screen. "Look, you can see right down there. At night you can tell if the outside light is on."

"I...definitely didn't know that." But it was true. He looked beyond Powell's finger and saw, with a sinking feeling he would not soon forget, part of the gravel drive and the entrance to his cottage, as if Powell had magically cleared a new sightline.

"Thought I heard something from down there, too," Powell said.

Oh, shit! Brian's sinking feeling became a free fall. How could he explain that he was tickling a guy almost to death?

"It was the next morning," Powell said. "Sounded like a car taking off, *fast.*"

Preparing himself for the worst, Brian forced himself to ask, "Did you hear...anything else?"

"Nope. Not a sound."

Powell's eyes were frank, innocent. Okay, so he wasn't toying with Brian. Still, he didn't dare look into those eyes for long, for even in their innocence they were deep enough to draw him into secret imagined places that sent chills along his spine. He mumbled something about having to get back to work, and hurried toward the refuge of the greenhouse.

Powell got into the habit of appearing on the porch at lunchtime. Brian didn't know what to make of it, any more than he knew what to make of some of the looks he caught Powell giving him. There the two of them were, sitting over sandwiches, Brian making a comment about one of the yard workers, what a good job he was doing on the lawn...and when he looked up, Powell was smiling with one eyebrow raised, as if Brian were really talking about...something else. Then the talk turned to other estate matters, and Brian realized what a task Powell had taken on, practically running the whole place all by himself.

"Let me know," Brian said, "if there's anything I can help you with."

Was that a smile playing at Powell's lips again? And what was there to smile about?

Everything came to a head when, over the course of two days, Brian was subjected to two sights that just about drove him over the edge.

The yard crew was mowing the lower part of the estate—

Brian could hear a mower approaching the cottage late one afternoon, when he had just got back from the greenhouse. He was surprised to hear the engine cut off not far from his door. Then the doorbell rang.

It was a young man he had noticed before—a good worker, very conscientious about trimming around the trees and hedges. And he was also—how could Brian fail to notice?—extremely attractive, all the more so when he was standing right there on the cottage stoop, wiping his sweaty forehead with the back of his wrist. It was one of the hottest days they'd had yet, so he was working without a shirt. And, Brian quickly noticed, he was barefoot too.

"I'm sorry to bother you," he said. "I was wondering if I could get some water."

"Of course. Come in." Brian stepped aside. "Please, help yourself."

The young man stood at the sink drinking his tumbler of water while Brian watched. Oh, how he watched this well-built, half-naked man in low-riding khaki shorts, his big bare feet at right angles to each other on the linoleum. After emptying his glass he filled it again, giving Brian more time to look. That narrow waist leading so gracefully to a slim but powerful-looking chest, that wink of armpit as he raised the glass higher...and those *feet*.

Brian's fingers twitched.

"Thanks," the man said, setting the glass carefully in the sink. He wiped his mouth with the back of his wrist. "What's your name?"

"B-Brian." He nearly ran to the door to open it. "Look, I don't mean to rush you, but I was in the middle of something...."

"Oh. Sure." The young man took his leave, flashing a particularly sweet smile at Brian as he passed.

Brian closed the door and sank down against it till his butt hit the floor. He had to do something—something, that is, beyond his immediate goal of beating off while he pictured that young stud, the way he had looked standing at the sink in his bare feet. But what, what could he do?

Then there was Powell, the very next day—Powell on the screened porch at lunchtime, finishing his sandwich, swiping at his mouth with a napkin, and reaching out with his leg to drag the ottoman close to his chair. Brian was always conscious of Powell's feet—size 12, at least—and how they looked in the blue flip-flops that he often wore. Now Brian could hardly believe his eyes as Powell slid his feet from those flip-flops and planted them, naked, on the ottoman, almost close enough to touch. The soles of those luscious, dark brown feet were a light brown, almost pink, and Brian couldn't take his eyes off them. He could do so many things to them, and never get tired....

Suddenly he was aware that Powell was saying something... something important. "I'm sorry," Brian asked, "what were you saying?"

"I was saying that my schedule's going to change. I'm going away."

Away? "Oh, no...."

Powell smiled his crooked, slightly insinuating smile. "Don't worry, it's only for a long weekend. This coming weekend, in fact."

Brian tried to regain his composure. It wasn't easy, with those feet staring at him. "Well, uh...then you have to come over. For a drink?"

"I beg your pardon?"

Brian felt his face turning red. Was Powell offended? "I just mean, before you leave. Friday night. Come down to the cottage for a glass of wine, why don't you?" He couldn't believe he was saying this. He almost giggled, it sounded so unlike him.

Powell thought for a moment. "Well, I do need to tell you about a couple of things that might need handling while I'm gone. Nothing major, but still."

"Then it's settled! Eight o'clock?"

At the appointed time Brian had the Zinfandel on ice, and the two wineglasses that had been gathering dust at the back of his cupboard were washed and ready. He paced the length of the cottage, weight room to living room to bedroom and back, glancing at his watch every few seconds. Five minutes past eight. Now almost ten. He could have opened his front door and stood on the stoop to wait, but he didn't want to seem too anxious. Just when he thought he might have to turn on the TV to distract himself, or else lose his mind, the knock came at the door.

"Hello." Powell breezed in with his hands in the pockets of his navy blue shorts. His sweatshirt was half unzipped, revealing sculpted pecs. On his feet he wore silver cross-trainers with no-show socks—the kind that showed just enough. It made no sense, but it was sexy as hell.

"Well, hi," Brian said. He poured wine for the two of them, though he didn't know how he could drink any; he felt lightheaded already. "You're not leaving tonight, are you? I wouldn't want you to be drinking and driving."

"No, not until tomorrow."

"Good. Looks like it's going to storm soon, too."

"I hope so. We need the...relief."

Brian hoped his hand wasn't shaking too much as he took a large sip of wine. "Your family will be happy to see you."

"Oh, I don't have family anymore, really. I'm just going back to the old place to look around. So I can take my time, there's no one expecting me."

"No one's expecting you...." Brian was *definitely* light-headed. "Oh, sorry, I didn't give you your glass...*oops!*" Wine splashed onto Powell's sweatshirt. "Oh, I'm so sorry! At least it's not red wine. Here, let me help you." Before Powell could move Brian was unzipping his shirt. "Why don't you slip this off so we can let it dry?" Scarcely believing he had the balls to do it, he helped Powell remove the sweatshirt and draped it over the back of a kitchen chair. Then he turned to confront the most beautiful male torso he'd ever seen. It wasn't a matter of working out like a maniac; you had to be born with a body like that. And smooth...did Powell shave his chest and abs? "Please, sit down," Brian said, his voice husky with desire, warning him that he needed to be cool or he would drive this breathtaking man away. He cleared his throat several times before saying, "I'll pour you another glass."

"Sure." Powell wasn't shy about making himself at home, leaning back in the large recliner till the footrest popped up. Brian looked forward to getting another look at his feet, even if they were encased in cross-trainers. Powell surprised him, though, by bending his knees to get at the laces of first one shoe, then the other. He pried them off, letting them fall to the floor. Then he peeled off the white no-show socks, letting them fall to the floor too.

Brian had to set down his glass, his hand was shaking so

much. There were *the feet*, propped up right in front of him, almost within reach. Those pale, almost pink soles were immaculate, with no trace of callus. They were lovingly tended to, the skin kept soft, smooth…. "That recliner goes back another notch," Brian said, no longer worrying about the huskiness of his voice. Powell wasn't worried either. He moved the recliner's lever once more and leaned back into a near-horizontal position. Now Brian had a better view, not only of those gorgeous feet but of Powell's whole package—his inner thighs, the generous mound of his crotch, those abs, the rib cage expanding above them like a vast, tender structure begging for assault. If only he would raise his arms so that Brian could see his armpits.

And just like that, Powell raised his arms, lacing his fingers together behind his head, the picture of relaxation…and vulnerability. How Brian loved the sight of those armpits, recesses just made for fingers and tongue! He loved the tightly coiled hair in those pits, too, but if he had his way he'd shave it off, make that tender skin all the more susceptible to prolonged stroking and poking. *Was* Powell ticklish? Oh, he *had* to be! It would a shame for this body to be insensitive in any way. The man was made to be played with.

The silence between them lasted for a minute or so. Powell carefully reached for the wineglass on the table beside his chair, and just as carefully brought it to his lips. Drinking in his nearly horizontal position was difficult, and a few drops of wine spilled from the corner of his mouth. Instinctively he sought them with his tongue, and it was the sight of that tongue, and those wet, parted lips, that drove Brian over the edge—drove him right out of his chair and onto the recliner in one desperate leap.

The chair was sturdy enough to bear both of them, and roomy enough for Brian to straddle his victim without crowding. He went for the ribs first, learning in a fraction of a second the answer to the question he'd spent so many hours pondering. Yes, Powell was ticklish, extremely so—oh, dyingly so! At the first touch of his ribs he shouted, bringing his arms down so fast that his elbow clipped Brian in the nose. Unfazed, Brian moved to those abs that were just begging to be prodded. Powell wasn't about to stay still for any of this; he began flailing, knees and elbows pumping, hands pushing against any part of Brian he could reach.

Brian had known all along that, if Powell proved to be as ticklish as Brian dreamed he'd be, there would be a fight, a prolonged one. He'd get beaten, scratched, bitten and bruised. But the fight was worth whatever it took to bring this sexy man down; any pain that he felt would make it that much sweeter when his powerful opponent finally fell! Summoning all of his own muscle power, Brian moved in, dodging the panicky flailing of arms and legs, keeping his eyes on that tender ticklish midsection. Finally he managed to pin Powell's right arm with his knee, and Powell's left arm over his head. Thus Powell's naked left side was exposed, and Brian took full advantage, his free hand darting from Powell's waist to his side to his ribs to his armpit. Powell lost all self-control, dissolving into helpless, full-throated laughter that was the most beautiful sound Brian had ever heard. Holding Powell's arm at bay was like trying to keep a bear trap open, but Brian kept tickling, never tiring of grabbing at meaty, responsive flesh. His persistence paid off as Powell's great shivering strength began to bleed away. He was just too ticklish to resist, especially with his own howling laughter weakening him too. "That's it," Brian said. "Give in, baby, let it happen, 'cause it's going to happen anyway." As Powell turned his head to the side and howled, Brian brought his mouth close to his ear and said, "I'm gonna tickle you for a long, *long* time!"

It couldn't last forever, though, on the recliner, with so much of their combined weight pressing against its back. When it finally tipped over Powell did a near-somersault, his feet flying, while Brian managed to land on his hands and knees. The chair was probably broken, the table smashed, and the wineglass had spiraled its contents all over the carpet. But Brian didn't give a fuck, because one of Powell's feet was *right there*, in front of his face, and before Powell could even try to collect himself Brian was clutching that naked foot close, finding its silken sole to be as addictive as it looked. He wanted to tickle it forever, thoroughly, maddeningly, teaching his fingers and nails and tongue to move in a million new ways. Powell lay flat on his back and howled, unable to even try to sit up. Brian's hard-on pressed painfully against the carpet, and that was all right because he knew he was going to come, and come and come.... Powell would, too. One look back gave Brian a good view of the tent pole rising in Powell's shorts.

Time got away from Brian, as it tended to do when he was tickling. When his fingers began to cramp he let his mouth take over, licking, sucking and nibbling that squirming foot, deliriously wedging his tongue-tip between the toes as sweat poured down his face. Powell had all but stopped struggling, his laughter weakening. Good, good! He was almost ready for the bed.

Brian got to his knees and pinned his victim's ankles between them, which gave him both soles to work on at once. If one of those soles was heaven, then the sight, smell and feel of both of them together nearly made Brian faint. His fingers sped like mad across that flesh, as Powell's roars grew almost pathetic, hoarse and straining. He'd reached that wonderful stage where it took all of his energy to try to draw enough breath to keep his insane laughter going. If Brian was a tickling machine then Powell was a tickled machine, unable to do anything but express his ticklishness and then, finally, surrender to it....

That time was coming. Exhausted and trembling, Brian released Powell's feet only when his knees began to ache from his crouched position. Turning, he saw the nearly naked length of Powell sprawled, delirious, on the carpet: a vision too lush, too sensual, and too fucking *hot* to be true. But if this was a dream, then he was going to live out every precious second of it. He crawled toward Powell's upper body and, lying on his side, pressed his fingertips into Powell's armpits and let them play. Powell responded with a grin of pure agony, and laughter so shrill, so hysterical, that Brian felt a mighty heaving in his midsection, his cock pulsing in his shorts, shooting out cum.

When he recovered, he brought his voice close to Powell's ear. "Can you hear me?"

Powell's crazy grin kept coming and going. He was panting like a dog now, and seemed unaware that, for the moment anyway, he wasn't being tickled. "Listen to me," Brian said. "Are you listening? *Listen*, or I'll tickle you to death right now!"

Powell's eyes opened wide. He seemed unsure of where to look, as if Brian's voice could be entering his confused mind from anywhere. When he turned his head and found Brian's face *right there,* his eyes opened even wider and he began trembling. "Don't worry," Brian said, wishing he hadn't made that tickle-to-death remark: Powell was in too fragile a state for that. Yes, this strong and capable man, who managed the estate practically all by himself—the Powell who had brazenly displayed his body while washing the car, who had propped his bare feet so confidently in Brian's face—was now reduced to a panic-stricken mass of lethally ticklish flesh. "Don't worry," Brian said again. "You'll be all right, but you have to do *exactly* what I say. Do you understand?" Powell nodded, but his eyelids drooped as if he might succumb to exhaustion now that his tickling torment had ceased. "We need to get to the bedroom," Brian said. "You're too heavy for me to carry, you have to get there under your own steam. It's not that far, so start crawling."

Powell just looked at him, an overwhelming question in his eyes: *Are you gonna tickle me to death?*

"I said, start crawling." Brian returned to those ribs he now knew so well. There were two spots, one on either side of the rib cage, that could make Powell do anything. He'd fucking *fly* to keep those spots from being touched. All he had to do now, though, was crawl, and so he managed, under the threat of rib-torture, to haul himself up onto his hands and knees. "That's good, now get moving," Brian said. Powell stayed stuck in position. "*Or else,*" Brian added. With an agonized grunt Powell began to move forward. They made an enjoyably strange procession, one man on his hands and knees, the other beside him on his knees, his fingers floating just above the other man's ribs. Then the sight of Powell's rump in the air was too tempting for Brian to resist; he slid his hand under the waistband of Powell's shorts—not an easy feat, those shorts being tightly stretched as they were by the big man's boner—and let his finger play with Powell's asscrack. Powell halted, arched his back—in terror or pleasure? "Has a man ever touched you there before?" Brian whispered. "Tell me you like it, please tell me you like it." Powell lifted his rear, making it easier for Brian to find his asshole. Brian's finger slid deep. He lowered his head to kiss the base of Powell's spine.

"We've got a lot more to do," he said.

Powell was flat on his back in Brian's bed, his mouth open, staring at the ceiling. Using his soft restraints, Brian had fastened his victim's wrists and ankles to the bedposts—after removing his shorts and micro briefs—and now stood and stared, his mouth watering. "You've got the most beautiful cock I've ever seen." That fully erect staff strained halfway up Powell's belly toward his chest. A hard rain spattered the window, reminding him of Powell's earlier remark about relief. "You'll get your relief, and soon," Brian promised. "But first...you guessed it...." Naked, Brian crawled onto the bed. He would have to get to those feet soon, but now there was this glorious midsection, made more accessible with the shorts gone. He tested the slick, smooth area under Powell's navel. "You shave here, don't you?" Reaching for his handy bottle of oil, Brian anointed his fingers and let them play all over that groin, not forgetting to tease and torment his navel also. Powell, unable to talk, could still release that weak, shrill, hysterical giggling that was like an aphrodisiac. Brian closed his eyes, reveling in it, moving his hands up to Powell's sides, then toward his ribs, then back down again, to his powerful but ultraticklish thighs. When it was time to pay attention to that gorgeous dick and heavy hanging balls, Brian oiled up both hands and went to it. Powell, reduced to panting again, tossed his head wildly on the pillow. The tension gathering in his loins gained force, until at last he shot great streams of cum that nearly hit the ceiling. Brian's arm, face, chest, and shoulders were soaked, as were Powell's belly and chest. Using a hand towel, Brian mopped up as best he could. "That was quite a load, my friend. But I don't know if you're aware of this: ticklish guys tend to be even *more* ticklish after they shoot."

Powell's head was thrown back, his eyes closed. Had he passed out? More likely he just hadn't recovered yet from what might have been the most powerful orgasm of his life. Brian settled down at the end of the bed, next to an enormous, ticklish right foot. "I have to get out my tool kit," he said, "very soon." He was considering getting it now when the noise of the storm distracted him. Rain was striking the window with disturbing force. "What...?" Brian rose and approached the window. Was it his imagination, or did something *bounce* off the sill?

Hail. It was hail.

The greenhouse.

A wave of panic washed over him, even as he told himself not to worry. The greenhouse was old, with glass panes that weren't as hail-resistant as the newer plastics; but it would take tennis-ball-sized hail to inflict any damage, and nothing like that was happening here. Still, he couldn't take his eyes off the windowsill. Even the word *hail* was enough to jangle his nerves when he thought of the plants. "I have to go," he whispered. "I've got to check."

Powell, exhausted from hours of overstimulation, had fallen into a kind of toe-twitching sleep—as if he were still being tickled, but at a low enough intensity to allow for a much-needed escape from consciousness. Brian looked at the magnificent man with tears in his eyes: would he have to let him go? He couldn't leave him here, restrained, while he checked on the greenhouse...or could he? "I'll be right back," he whispered. "I promise."

The storm had already passed by the time he'd pulled on his jeans and T-shirt, but still he had to go, to check for damage. The thought of smashed panes and damaged plants made him sick. As he ran through the grass the hail crunched under his bare feet, confirming that he hadn't just imagined it. At the greenhouse it took him several tries to fit the key in the lock. He'd never been here in this state, his face and chest sticky with cum, his half-erect cock pressing against his jeans. At last the lock opened, and he stepped inside and touched the dimmer switch. He had hosed down the floor before leaving for the day to help keep the humidity high; that water had vaporized and there were no fresh puddles on the floor. Good. A quick look around showed nothing amiss, but he had to be sure. He took a flashlight from the utility closet, to get a more detailed look at the corners. Only after scanning the whitewashed glass again and again was he certain no breaks had occurred. He allowed himself to relax, feeling some of the tension drain from his shoulders as he leaned against a potting bench. Now he looked at the plants that had been silently observing him all this time. They often reminded him of the Roethke poem that described orchids with their "loose ghostly mouths." That image reminded him of Powell, too, in his tickling-crazed state. Brian had to get back, he'd been gone too long.

Running through the grass that was already losing its odd texture now that the hail was melting, he cursed himself for leaving the cottage in the first place, but what else could he have done? He burst through the front door, didn't bother to close it behind him as he crossed the living room in four leaping strides to the bedroom. What he saw there put a lump in his throat. He staggered against the straight chair by the window and sat down hard.

Powell was gone. He'd managed to work free from the restraints, which now hung from the bedposts like silent rebukes.

Brian's life was over—his life at the estate, anyway. He'd never be able to face Powell after this. With a sob he launched himself across the room to land flat on the bed, burying his face in the pillow, drinking in Powell's scent. He grabbed handfuls of sheet, still damp with sweat, and squeezed the fabric till his hands hurt, as if he could wring from it the very essence that was Powell.

When a knock came from the front door, Brian's heart nearly stopped. He saw how bad things could be: Powell had not only left, he'd called the police. "Come in!" Brian shouted. *Go ahead, take me away.*

Like so much of what had happened during the night, this didn't seem real: it was Powell standing in the bedroom doorway. He wore only his shorts, and his skin still glistened from exertion. And he looked younger, somehow—as if, in this cottage, he had been taken back to his first experience of how powerful sex could be; as if he had found in his tormentor an unexpected source of wonder. Almost shyly, he pushed a leather tote bag across the threshold with his bare foot.

"I had to get some things," he said, "if I'm going to stay here awhile."

DONUTS TO DEMONS

horehound stillpoint

Cruising craigslist, I've got my dick in hand, more than half hard, playing with my balls, tickling, working, getting that feeling going, you know, the urge mixed with the tingle, just loving the fact that I've got a cock, that it works, it gets hard; it's lickable, fleshy, thick enough and sturdy enough to get the salivary glands going for all the boys, men, studs, geniuses, and lovable losers I end up kissing, licking, sniffing, sucking, et cetera, et cetera.

Jesus fucking Christ, I've seen every single cocksucker's picture on here a hundred thousand times already. Fuck this shit. There's nobody here for me. At least a third of these guys are just looking for pics, more than half will only reply to a specific, professional, porno-worthy image, and another third don't have a firm grip on reality.

Bad math. No solution.

Still, my cock swells heavy with hope. My balls don't rule my life, but when they're this full, this heavy, this alive, they run the show for a few hours, I guess. My butt has needs, too. And my nipples. My tongue. My mouth. My big ol' bicycle-built thighs. Hell, even my toes want to rub up against some guy's calves. My whole body feels like a sex organ sometimes.

I want some bruiser licking my armpits.

A meaty, musty ass on my face…on my chest, while I blow him…then his ass sitting down on my dick, riding my pole while I push up to heaven…wraparound legs…nips to suck on and play with…shoulders that can pick up and carry the world…a chest to rest on afterward.

I want…

Great. Another fifty-four-year-old advertising for somebody under twenty-five. And another UB2-spouting manbot. More breed-my-hole, BB, anonymous-pounding, door-open, no-talking, greedy, mindless assholes. No fucking thanks.

Excuse me, but I want a guy with a mind, 'cause it's sexy when a man can talk about real things. It's sexy when he can laugh at himself, at conditions on Spaceship Earth. To me, it's a turn-on when a man can talk about his spirituality and not come off as a loser-idiot. It's hot when he doesn't have to get drunk, or fucked up, to get on his knees and show what he can do, with no hesitation and completely shameless. Hairy or smooth, muscular or wiry, geeky or cool, young and tight or mature and comfortable with imperfections: I want—not to coin a phrase or anything—a man.

Wait a minute: what have we here?

The Fortress. San Francisco's finest dungeon is having a Dark Night, as in lights out, allowing our inner monsters to come out and play?

Fan-fucking-tastic!

Ah shit, shit, goddammit. It's not tonight; it's February 16, four nights from now. Fuck.

Crap.

Screw it.

Breathe.

Okay, it's okay, but craigslist, you and I are done. For now.

Bye-bye, Internet. Funkadelic on the stereo. Chair into reclining position. It's beatin' off time.

Which folder tonight: Creamrising, or Dreamangels, or...

Picsajerks, let's go.

You, college wrestler, with your semihard cock showing in your singlet. You're up. You, trucker, standing there in your underwear, getting a blow job in the shadows, with your buns looking tight and your back as broad as all outdoors. Yep. You too, drunken frat boy with your floppy balls and fat snake cock falling out of your boxers, with that smirky grin on your face, knowing goddamn well what we want. Mechanic, yeah, you too, with your hard-on in one hand and a monkey wrench in the other, major tools. Phone repairman, in someone's backyard, talking to a supervisor or something while getting sloppily sucked off by a customer who doesn't give a shit about his reputation or his neighbors. Swimmer, squeezing the boner in your swim trunks. Locker room guy, adjusting your jockstrap. Other locker room guy, bending over and giving everyone your ass. You guys make me feel like the whole world is hot, horny and ready to blast off. You convince me the wave that's coming to bury us all is not Armageddon, not Global Warming, not war and racism and voracious corporations and jingoistic nation/religions; no, the wave that's coming is Come, a Kingdom of Come, an ocean, a cosmic sea, an eternal moment of supremely satisfying joy. I don't have to come right now because I will drink it all in and swallow and swim and drown and die of Come and be reborn in Come and reside in the source, the original waters, where there is nothing to desire and everything is one.

Plus, it's fun to edge with my two-dimensional heroes.

Thanks, guys. You let your pictures be taken and we are grateful. We needed you and you stepped forward. You guys have given rise to thousands of boners and gallons of splooge, and there's plenty more where that came from.

Wait.

Friday night will be here in two shakes of a tail feather and the wink of an eye.

Well, slap my ass and call me Lucky. I did not think that table was going to double tip me. The people there looked at the check for a long time. I try to be a decent waiter and play by the rules, so I put two stars beside the word SERVICE on the check and then underlined the amount of the tip (since we are allowed to add gratuity to any table of six or more). How can anyone miss that? If a customer fails to pay the slightest attention to the bill, it is not my fault. And if I end up with an extra fifty dollars tonight, I know right where it's going.

Master J's Leather Store.

For those latex shorts.

With the wraparound zippers.

The men at the Fortress are going to see me coming around

the corner Friday night, now that I can justify spending money on something as unnecessary as latex shorts that make me look like I'm hung like a horse. They're so tight, they feel like part of my skin, so that when the zipper gets pulled open and air hits flesh, it feels as though it's me who is being opened up. It feels as though this body has brand new holes that need to be fiddled with, wetted down, and filled up. And when the zipper is opened in the back, well, it feels as though the foundation of the Universe might be cracking open. And that Monster Wave of Come I imagine flipping me over like the *Poseidon*—I can practically feel it already, only it ends up lapping gently at my port side, because I am free, I am not separate, I am made of Come, and I am that big, I can take loads and loads and loads, I can take it all.

I can take everything laid at my doorstep.

Lord have mercy, there's Dimitri. I did not expect to see him here at Master J's Leather Store, which proves what an idiot I am. He works here. Fuck, he looks good. He plants himself so straight and tall, so upright, everything about him looks to be standing at attention. Including his nipples. And the bulge in his jeans. His long, strong legs. He's African-American but something about his face puts me in mind of Egyptian nobility. I don't know what to call his haircut, but he's so sleek and finished, he might as well be a statue come to life.

He's a real gentleman, extremely intelligent, sexy as hell, with an intact sense of humor, and capable of listening as well as talking. Plus, he volunteers to do important, selfless, good works on the other side of the world. I know all this because we dated for a few weeks a couple of months ago.

It was December of last year when I met Dimitri for the first time. I had gone into Master J's Leather Store to buy a cock ring. Backtracking—again—for a moment: my old one had been removed by a wannabe–porn star at an underwear party. This bad boy, in the sheerest bikinis ever, said we could exchange rings even though we both had hard-ons. I judged that to be pretty near impossible. But he put my hands behind my head, leaned me up against a wall, and carefully proceeded to remove the donut—my superthick, neoprene cock ring—not by easing my balls out, but by bending my dick gently, gently, and working the shaft out first. Then he really scared me. He told me he could put his steel cock ring on me, balls first, then smush my cockhead in and massage the rest of it all the way down in, and through. Yikes. But I kept my hands where he had put them, stuck my chest out, and let him go to town. It took about six minutes, I was so hard. He was too; our dicks were pointing straight up to the ceiling in the bar. Then he wanted me to do the same to him. Put my neoprene donut on him, balls first. His cock was about the same size as mine, a little thicker maybe; he said it would work fine, if I just had the patience. So I cupped his balls, lifted the neoprene, bent his dick a bit because it had to be done and he swore I would not hurt him, pointed the head into the donut hole, and spent the next ten minutes making a minor miracle happen.

Voila!

We laughed and joked about exchanging marriage vows now that we had put rings on each other. He told me he wanted to dance at a local porn theater on amateur night, and if I came to support him, he would treat me real good, and we could trade cock rings again. He promised to email me the next day about when and where to show up, and what fun we would have!

Of course I never got an email from him.

I can't say anything, though. Ninety percent of the time, I don't call the guys I say I'm going to call either. I want to, when I get the number. I mean to. Then, I don't. For one reason or another, I give up, or lose hope, or wait so long it would be awkward.

Hence, the visit to Master J's Leather Store, for another neoprene donut. I'm just not that fond of three-dollar steel cock rings. If you're going to be cheap, which I am, neoprene is the way to go.

The staff at Master J's lets you try on the cock rings, thank god. They didn't have the full-on donuts, but they did have nice thick neoprene rings of one-and-three-quarter-inch diameter.

So I made my nine-dollar purchase and guess who was at the cash register? He asked me if I wanted a small bag or did I intend to wear the cock ring out. I laughed and stuck my hands inside my loose heavy sweatpants and fumbled with the damn thing while I looked into this studly, beautiful, multiethnic leatherman's eyes.

"You need some help with that?"

I had visited Master J's infrequently but occasionally for some twenty-odd years, waiting and hoping and doing everything I could to get some guy to say those words...and then, when I least expected to hear them...

"Yeah! That'd be great," I enthused.

"Over here," he said, leading the way. He walked me to the dressing rooms. I ducked into one.

"This one," he suggested, pulling a large leather curtain to the side and opening the way into a double-sized changing room.

I pulled my sweats down, and my dick went: *boing!* Yep,

already hard. He put the cock ring on, the regular way, then he bent over, to work my balls in, and put my dick in his mouth. He got down on his knees and got serious, reaching up to tease, flick, and pinch my nipples, god love him. I always think that's such a generous thing to do. I reached down and returned the favor. We got busy, changing positions, trading blow jobs, and just having a blast.

Then, he said, "Wait here a minute. I'll be right back."

Good timing: I needed to catch my breath. He had probably done this once or twice before (I even saw lube up on the ledge, along with a roll of paper towels), but I'd been waiting for this for two decades.

He returned right before I could get bored or uncomfortable.

"Try these on," he encouraged.

And he handed me the aforementioned latex shorts.

"I think these will fit you."

You have to work to get those fuckers on, but man, it is absolutely worth the effort.

"Now see, the zipper goes all the way from the front to the back. Plus, you got four tabs. So you can unzip the front and close it back up from the top, while you—or somebody else—does the same in the back. That wide flap of latex inside keeps your little hairs from getting caught in the zipper. Let me show you."

He put me on this small round pedestal in the dressing room, turned me around, and opened the zipper in the dead center of my butt, whereupon I nearly swooned, especially when his tongue got to licking and darting around my asscheeks and then in between. He went to work on my crack and got my asshole so wet, I had to bite my tongue to keep from begging him to fuck me right then and there.

Truth is, orally, I'm superslut, whereas anally, I'm a scared schoolmarm.

I have to be partially or at least somewhat in love, to fuck. Top or bottom. I mean, we don't have to be forking over the down payment on a wedding cake or anything, but love has to be on the table. It has to be in the room as a possibility, the sparkling glittery promise of love, a relationship, a slim chance at least that we might conceivably have a future. I have fucked exactly three guys in the last fifteen years and they were all extremely talented bottoms, charming, lovable, and determined. None of these turned out to be my next husband, however. One, unbeknownst to me, already had a husband: groan. One lived on the other side of the planet: sigh. And one did not share a single interest in my rock 'n' roll-artfag-into-Eastern-spirituality-world: alas.

Exactly one guy has fucked me in the past fifteen years and he was a top who turned out to be as patient and gifted and generous as he advertised on Craigslist. That was an experiment, to see if I could still take a dick up my butt after so much time. Love was not in the room in that instance, and had no chance of appearing since Mr. Top, as good as he was at sex, was that bad at the art of conversation. I just wanted to get fucked because... well, just because. It did not make my toes curl with pleasure, but it wasn't horrible either, nor particularly painful.

That had happened three years before Dimitri escorted me into the dressing room, and I had not sought to repeat the event. So when Dimitri and his tongue and those latex shorts all conspired to make me feel like my asshole had suddenly turned into a pussy, my sirens went off. Which made me come before I could even send up a flare to let Dimitri know what was in the works. Our clothes were all over the floor so I aimed for my belly, which made me arch my back and that did signal my new buddy…but by the time he stood up and came around to face front, the show was over.

He dipped his finger into the pool of jizz that covered my abs, swirled it around and then popped that gooey finger into his mouth, just like a boy getting the last of the pudding.

Dimitri kissed me, stroked his cock for about twenty seconds, and creamed my already sticky belly while moaning into my open mouth. Now *that* just about made my toes curl, although I was standing on them at the time.

Obviously, we traded phone numbers before I left the store.

Not that I thought we would ever see each other again.

I did not buy the shorts at that time. Fun but too expensive. I left with my new neoprene cock ring, a wet spot forming in my briefs, and a smile I could not get off my face.

All of this, however, transpired three months ago, and in my world, in the gay world, hell, in any world, a lot can happen in three months.

We had, Dimitri and I, against the odds, gotten together again, in my apartment, for several sessions of superheated body-to-body contact mixed with gobs of oral sex and kissing. We did not fuck. We talked, a little, after we both came, but still our association constituted more of a fuck buddy situation than a boyfriend relationship.

I wanted more.

I started calling him, almost daily. Even if he hadn't returned my call from the previous day, I found myself dialing his number. That last time I called him was New Year's Eve; he wasn't where he had said he would be or we got our signals crossed or something. I felt disappointed, even humiliated, and decided not to call again. He didn't call either.

To make myself feel better, I went over in my mind the details of his previous visit, and then I extrapolated and envisioned a whole story from that point on.

The last time we had gotten together in my apartment, he had been extremely gloomy. About his job. About his best friend at that job leaving under unhappy circumstances. About other things as well. I could only get a few sentences out of him, actually. We had sex as therapy that time.

I thought maybe he had quit his job. Maybe he had fallen into a serious depression. Maybe he was embarrassed, ashamed. Broke. It happens. I would have helped, but I didn't want to rescue any more boyfriends. Or fuck buddies. Doesn't work anyway.

I also don't want to be the only one pushing the relationship rock up the hill. We're both in it, or I'm letting it roll right back down into the valley, and walking away.

So in my mind, I walked away from Dimitri.

In the fantasyland in my head, he quit Master J's Leather Store and fell into a deep dark well, similar to the ones that have claimed other boyfriends, lovers, fuck buddies. I erased how happy I had felt with him; erased the memory of sex that had been on the verge of lovemaking; erased the feeling of muscles and skin, eyes and lips that contained the air of home…all the things the most sizzling sex with the hottest stranger in the city cannot provide.

This is how I could be so surprised to see Dimitri in a store where I knew he worked.

Far from depressed, embarrassed, or broke, Dimitri looks amazingly eager to take care of me.

"Hey, Dimitri."

"Greg. Good to see you."

I grin.

He smolders. In a good way.

"I got an extra fat tip last night, so I came back for those latex shorts."

"Oh, yeah. The ones with the wraparound zippers."

The quick smile I got made my balls tingle.

"They're over here."

We take a short walk. He doesn't even look at the stock on the rack, just sticks his hand out, lifts the hanger from its little hook, and presents.

"These are the ones," he assures me. "You know where the dressing room is. Try them on again, and I'll be back there in a minute."

It's just like the first time, only better.

With a bottle of water in my hand and sporting the rock 'n' roll look that still gets guys thinking with their cocks, I hit the patio-cum-back room of one of the seediest gay bars in the world, and hit the jackpot. A buddy's there, a guy I know even though I can't remember his name, and he's already working his crotch, just waiting for one green light, which I am more than happy to provide. Both of our dicks are out in minutes, and they are not alone. Guys stroll over and start blowing him, me, whomever. Guys are pulling on our tits, tickling our balls, licking our butts. He and I are staring each other down, making good old-fashioned porno faces.

Neither one of us is a *Yeah, work that shaft, cocksucker* dirty-talk kind of guy; we do it with our energy, which by now is bouncing off the grimy wooden slats which pass for walls around here.

I shoot; some guy takes it on the chin. The guy licking my ass backs away to watch. My friend a few feet away comes all over a chesty dude's shoulder and we are all of us gone to seed.

"Hey, motherfuckers..." the bartender shouts through a tiny, barred window near his ice machine. "The sex club is down the street, you assholes. They charge twenty-five dollars; why the hell should I let you guys do the same shit here for free?"

We smirk, or chuckle quietly, or act all sheepish; we were starting to buckle up anyway. The questions was rhetorical and the lecture was halfhearted at best. The T-shirts for this bar carry a legend that reads: RUINING REPUTATIONS FOR FIFTEEN YEARS.

They know which side of their toast has the butter. People don't come through the door of this bar for just a drink. They come to get their cocks sucked, or to watch someone else get his cock or ass worked over.

Still, it's an interesting question. Money aside, why don't we go to the neighborhood sex club?

Sex in a sex club: nothing could be more predictable. Sex in the back room of a bar—even a really seedy bar—that's bad-boy behavior, outlaw activity, rebel stuff. It practically takes us back to prehistoric, preverbal, good ol' days, as if me and my boyhood pal had just outrun a dangerous predator. We beat the beast and lived to tell the tale. How many times do we get to feel like that in the fucked-up America of the Twenty-first Century?

This is what I'm thinking while I put myself back together again. Zipping up, finishing my water, saying good-bye, grabbbing my backpack.

I get on my bike and start riding home, and it's a whole three or four minutes before I start thinking about Dimitri again.

He has disappeared. Again.

Every time I start to fall for him, he vanishes in a puff of smoke. Stops calling. Stops emailing.

Everything comes to a grinding halt, only there is no memo announcing the fact. I have to figure it out for myself.

Slowly.

As the days go by.

On top of it all, those stupid, goddamn, black latex shorts apparently carry some kind of fucking curse. I didn't get to wear them to the Fortress, because those Dark Nights are for Women Only. Some joker put it up on craigslist in the M4M category, who knows why. I also didn't get to wear them to a leatherman's soiree because I came down with pneumonia. When I recovered from that, I went back onto craigslist, but my year-old G-rated pics were not working for me. Coincidentally, a newly professional photographer had posted an offer for a free session in which someone could get hot new pics in two hours flat. He said he was just doing it to get more practice, working with various guys in random situations. When we met, he turned out to be quite a stud. Of course, the fucker insisted there would be no touching between us, which I agreed to, but then he put his hands in his pants, showing me what he wanted me to do, and asked if he could see the base of my cock, maybe I could pull my briefs down a bit, just a little more? He mentioned how I was giving him a hard-on, grabbing his jeans and proving his point. I got harder and harder and he asked me what I wanted to do, and before I knew it, I was beating off. He ended up taking seven hundred photos. He gave me a CD of them, swore up and down that they would not be used for anything...but I can't believe those pics will not end up in a magazine or on a website somewhere.

Especially since he got me to put on those motherfucking latex shorts. He got enough good shots to put a real layout together; didn't seem to me like he needed any practice, but what do I know.

Shit.

I have still never worn those shorts and played with anyone but Dimitri. They don't even make me feel horny anymore. They make me feel sad. Foolish. And alone.

Yes, loneliness has been creeping in. I like my apartment. I like being alone in my apartment, when I get home from the seedy bar with the dark, smoky patio. I've got all kinds of crazy shit to keep me company: *Cheap Thrills, The Idiot, Radio Ethiopia, Abraxas, Young Americans, Volunteers, Damned Damned Damned, To Bring You My Love, Born to Run, Sheer Heart Attack, Computer World, Too Much Too Soon, Todd, Mental Notes, Rattus Norvegicus, Entertainment!, The Grand Wazoo, Southern Nights, London Calling, Songs the Lord Taught Us,* and *Let's Get It On.* (Not to mention stuff like *Tweedles, Giant Robot, Black Acetate,* and *Opera Tuna Teen Ox).*

I've got paintings on practically every square foot of wall space; it's a riot of color, my cozy downtown studio. I've got homemade coleslaw, organic potato chips, Dubliner cheese, homemade tuna salad (chunky white tuna—dolphin safe— lemon mayo, oregano, parsley, garlic, celery, carrots, onion, apple—all finely diced, of course—a little mustard, and fresh ground pepper), plus seeded spelt crackers and coconut macaroons, all of which is thoroughly delicious to a health-food nut like me. The books on the shelves range from Genet to Anne

Lamott, with plenty of room for Beckett, McMurtry, Wolfe, Dostoyevsky, Hornby, Vonnegut, sci-fi favorites Rudy Rucker and Robert J. Sawyer, and miraculously talented writer-friends like Michelle Tea, Lynn Breedlove, Kirk Read, Justin Chin, Carol Queen, Ian Philips, Greg Wharton, and Daphne Gottlieb. I've got *Kill Bill* and *Funny Girl*, *Amadeus* and *Batman Begins*, *Shaun of the Dead*, *A Star Is Born* (the Judy Garland and James Mason version, thank you very much), *Spun*, *Priscilla*, and *Trick*.

Oh my god, I almost forgot to include *Kung Fu Hustle* and *Angels in America*. Shoot me.

But goddamn, it gets quiet when a man has made his presence felt here and then suddenly stops visiting.

I wanted to share my stuff with Dimitri. I did get to read him something by my poetry brother Trebor Healey. No matter what it does to my poor prose, I need to quote the first few lines of "Krsna" to render a taste, else no one will believe Dimitri's reaction.

Cobalt-cocked blueboy
Gopi fucker
I wanna fuck you till you're blue...

Dimitri started breathing weird when he heard this, and he spoke in these broken phrases, like a man in shock from seeing something too bright for his eyes.

"How did he do that?

"Each line is like its own hard-on...

"But it's transcendent, at the same time...

"I feel high just from hearing it."

When he added, "Let's read it again," I took the first step on the path to falling in love with Dimitri. In spite of all my caution and past hurts and scar tissue and uber-fear, my heart opened up and experienced a feeling which in words could only be described as *At last*.

It was not enough. Apparently. Unbelievably. Not enough.

He didn't stick around. He went back into the woodwork.

I'm sure he has reasons, but that doesn't do me much good.

I want a man with staying power.

I want a man who feels like home.

I want to fuck again and have it mean something.

I want all of me to be in bed with the guy, my guy, and I want all of him in there too. The good, the bad, the hard-core ugly, and the healing radiance of love. I want it all, with tons of laughter on top. Corny stuff. Beyond corny. The cliche that refreshes the whole world.

I want it.

I want Dimitri.

In our last conversation, Dimitri confesses, as casually as possible, that he has demons he must face before he and I… unfortunately, that sentence never gets finished.

"Yeah, well, I could probably name your demons right now."

"Yes, you probably could."

In the moment, I'm thinking of the usual suspects: ego, low self-esteem, fear of intimacy, guardedness. Later on, when I was alone, I got to reflecting that Dimitri might be one of the best human beings I've ever met, but he's still only human, and that's a demon or three right there.

He's male. That's at least one more.

He's American.

Gay.

Black.

While we're on this winning streak, let's add in a violent childhood. Incest. Rape. Gangs. A shot in the chest before he even got to his teenage years (thank god it didn't kill him, thank god it only left him with a totally butch scar that I would have been happy to kiss day after day). All of which Dimitri has mentioned previously, briefly, minimally, with the least amount of emotion possible.

It's a miracle he didn't turn into a criminal. Hell, he doesn't even dress like a thug. He's an upstanding, life-affirming, tax-paying, San Francisco leatherman.

I want to suck his dick till the day I die.

I'm not sure that's how the story is going to end, though. I'm not sure I like my chances. Every day without a call or an email seems like a day in which this bright beautiful light of real happiness fades further and further into a dark forest.

I know these woods. This unhappy place.

The thicket and the brush of my stupid thoughts.

The dry twigs I smoke to forget. The smelly swamp of depression. The worm-riddled logs of negative self-esteem. The loneliness of the territory and the night. The rocks of anger picked up along the path. The isolation as the forest closes in.

Fuck yeah, I know it.

Pretty soon, it's not so easy to see your way clear. You can't recognize the most familiar landmarks.

You forget you were ever on a path.

A familiar fog settles in.

Quicksand everywhere.

Desperate days.

Last-ditch efforts.

I don't know what to do...except the only thing I know how to do.

Write.

Get busy, get it down and send it out. All this.

Everything. (No, not everything, not really, not by a long shot; I left out some important bits and pieces. Like my failure in bed with Dimitri that one time. My health problems. The fact that I'm no longer clean and sober. I omitted as much of the buzz-kill stuff as possible. Neuroses. My neediness. The shit that doesn't get anyone's dick hard. I did my best soft-shoe razzle-dazzle around all the issues and baggage and fucked-up indelicacies that we log on to craigslist.com to forget about in the first place. And if I could have made my story cleaner and hotter and more suitable for pulling your putz, trust me, I would have.)

Dimitri did say, freely and unequivocally, I could write about him. He said I didn't have to change any details, or hide his identity or anything. He said he would be honored to have me write about him.

Okay.

Tomorrow I will do a copy and paste of this little document, and send it to him. I don't know what else to do. I already used my second-to-last gambit: the invitation for him to join me at the Warfield for the Iggy and the Stooges reunion tour. He was momentarily speechless, then stoicly excited, when I originally told him I had two tickets for us to go. I reminded him of it, in an email, a few days ago.

Nothing. Not a word from the guy I wanted to call my man.

So I don't have a lot of hope.

I mean, Iggy. Chance of a lifetime to see the original Stooges. On Iggy's birthday. It's gonna be crazy and it's gonna be sublime.

Didn't get a rise out of my buddy, though.

Anyhow, this is my story, this is my truth; this is all I've got, what I'm down to, my very last dime.

Come on, Dimitri. The forest is closing in on the path, demons are on the move, and night is gathering.

And if some other dear reader sees me a few months from now sucking some stranger's cock, have a heart, will ya? Say hi, say something funny, put a hand on my shoulder, throw me a lifeline.

I might be drowning in an ocean of Come, after all.

ORANGE

Lee Houck

Step one: Pick a moment in your life. Press your finger down onto it, holding it like you would the first loop in a square knot. Step two: Find a moment that represents where you are now, something separate, current and different, and touch another finger to that, too. Step three: Measure the distance from one to the other—in lovers lost, furniture stolen from street corners, estimated electric bills paid, early morning phone solicitations, car accidents you witnessed. Band-Aids on fingers. Step four: Figure out how the hell you got here now from where you were then.

Sometimes the first moment I choose is my cheesy orange fingertips in the propped-open back end of a station wagon parked on the tire-tracked sand of a crowded Florida beach.

I must have been three years old. I don't remember it, but I have seen the photograph of me sitting there—blue and yellow tub of Cheese Balls between my diapered legs, hand stuck inside. Blond hair, just like now. When you look at pictures of yourself doing things that you don't remember, the image freezes and becomes part of your history, even though it seems invented. A memory that forms who you are without you knowing it. Like genes, unconscious but familiar.

Sometimes the moment is foamy orange Circus Peanuts melting on the dashboard of a pickup truck. We were driving there without any place to be, or any place in mind to end up in. He bought a Mountain Dew because it was my favorite. I should tell you about the way his hands moved when he talked. The way words seemed to burst out of his fingers. The urgency, the way he made even garbage seem like quantum physics. But it all gets screwed around in my brain. Memory serves only to fuck things up. And photographs can lie to you, because if you have a picture of someone, and he goes away, dies or disappears, the photo becomes the only thing you remember about him.

How did this start?

Shredded carrots at a salad bar, on some school trip in a shopping mall?

A completely mediocre, but still your favorite, orange-tinted album cover?

The smooth spine of an unread paperback book?

Other times, like this time right now, right here in this guy's bedroom, it's greasy orange cleanup wipes, the kind that he rubbed up and down his arms before climbing up behind me. "Do you like to get fucked?" he says.

A giant of a man, six foot plus something. Huge, but not

alien-looking, still handsome, still attractive. A tiny line of mustache. He's bulky like a sack of flour, his body dense, smooth like rising dough. Forearms thick as a coffee can, covered in what I guess is car grease or engine grime, a shiny ultraviolet glimmer. Smells like steel. Skin brown underneath.

His lips are drawn on so beautifully that I can't help but look right into his mouth when he's talking, and not into his eyes. He kisses my hand.

He's holding a white plastic tub. Tearing off the lid, he pulls out a strip of creamy orange-colored cheesecloth. A powerful knock-your-ass-on-the-floor kind of scent. The most fake, plastic, outer space, movie-smelling orange. Good though. The orange-powered grease cutter is pasted into the spaces of the cheesecloth. He rubs his hands, detailing the knuckles, the cuticles. And the smell of it hangs around through the entire act. Through the rough fingers, unclipped nails tugging at my warm knot of skin, before he's climbing up behind me.

Once again, I end up on my stomach. And I realize that when he reaches his arm around my face, around my neck, and grabs on to my shoulder with his hand—starting to really fuck me hard—that I'd better get fucking control of myself. I start to flatten out. In my head, I mean. I start finding that preaware, rocklike place where I can concentrate. I go to the place where everything is flat. I'm inhaling, looking for that sugary ashy smell, and suddenly, uncontrollably, my brain begins its hyper-journey back to twelve years old. Memories hijack my neurons. Memories of taste, of touch, of fake orange, and when I place my mouth on this guy's arm, it all becomes clear. I'm no longer in this place, in this bedroom. My head, my brain, myself, it's all somewhere entirely different.

We're pushing our bikes up this giant hill, and the bugs

are swarming around our heads. Hot Southern summer, with salty beads of sweat around our brows and upper lips. Slapping our necks with our dusty hands, smashing black gnats. Sometimes one will fly into your mouth. But we don't care when they do. And when we get to the top of the hill we find a beat-up old cassette tape, cracked open and spilling its threads of sound onto the pavement. And we unwind the tape, a huge, hundred-foot string. And we snap it in half at the middle, tying the pieces onto the seats of our bikes, and ride back down the hill, watching the glittering of who knows what on cassette flowing behind us like a tail, like a stretched-out wish, like a thin brown destiny.

We're driving a beat-up white car through a rainstorm at three o'clock in the morning in the middle of Mississippi—or maybe we'd made it to Alabama without seeing the sign, or maybe we were still in Louisiana. And the rain is coming down so hard that we can't see the street in front of us. And we're both thinking *tornado warning for upper and lower Alabama*, but we don't say it out loud. So for three hours we travel what adds up to be forty-two miles on the low-shoulder freeway. We pass a few cars parked on the side, determined to wait it out. And in those three hours; the loud, wind-shaken hours; we don't speak. I squint, my eyes low along the top of the dash, and he drives, tapping the gas pedal, not braking, easing on, rolling back toward home. Then, crossing the state line, we see the brightness of the morning. I look over at him, he stares ahead.

And when he loosens his grip around my neck, around my head, when my mouth breaks free from the inside of his elbow, the awfulness of the present returns. This guy, this orange-smelling grease monkey, barks in my ear about how he wants to tie me up. Haven't I heard all this before? You would think it was tattooed across my forehead: TIE ME UP, TIE ME UP!

He knots my hands to the bed frame, rope made of something natural, cotton I think. Blocks my legs apart with a short two-by-four. So I'm spread-eagle on this bed, on my stomach, of course, and the knots rub raw places into my wrists. And I know that if I didn't tug so much on the rope, then it wouldn't rub so much. But he asks me to struggle a little, and I don't know how much is a little. So I do it until he starts going, "Yeah, yeah."

We used to take drives out to nowhere on weeknights. He'd smoke and we'd put a mix tape on and take turns talking. About what we wanted to do when we grew up, even though we were sixteen and didn't know what we wanted to do when we grew up. And didn't really care. And what we wanted to do would change every few miles, every few minutes. And we were grown up already. We'd pass rusted farm machinery, crumbling frames jutting out of the browning grass, leaping out of the dirt. Out near the deserted factory that you'd ride past if you went far enough. He'd take pictures of me in front of it. He wouldn't let me take pictures of him, he said he didn't like having his picture taken. I wouldn't smile because I knew what we were doing was serious. And he knew it was serious. And so he didn't ask me to smile. We didn't have to pretend. It was too hard to pretend. And mostly it still is.

We were fifteen and hiking up the part of the trail that was marked DO NOT ENTER. Because the best parts of the mountain were marked DO NOT ENTER. We'd stand at the tip of the rock, where the trail went shooting straight out into the air, over the waterfall, the canopy. The place where red-tailed hawks spiraled in circles, heavy wings lifted by the fast and beautiful air. The place where he put his arm on my shoulder. And we stood quiet. I could hear the thumping of my heartbeat in my ears, in my chest, in the tingling pulsing pressure of my fingertips. Some nights we slept outside in heavy nylon sacks, drowning in the half-light of the moon. Some nights we climbed trees, or burned pine-needle shapes in the road. Picked blueberries and ate them in the dark.

And I see him pull open the bedside table drawer, noticing the grease mark he missed on the back of his elbow. The orange air is thick and clammy around my head, stuck inside my nose, taking my olfactory canals hostage. He opens the drawer, rustles through the dog-eared *TV Guide*, the (what is that, a compact?) the Q-Tips and wadded up tissues. He pulls out a syringe. And the needle goes down into the side of my arm, a warm yellow energy flushing out my veins. If pain and happiness were mixed together and held in liquid suspension, that'd be almost what it felt like. And here's where everything comes slamming back into me, tearing open the little fear pockets in my head. I jerk hard on my wrists and there's nothing. No response. Like waking up too fast and you fall down. Only here the falling feels so fucking good. All of a sudden, falling without impact. So I slam my face back into the pillow, like a fool trying to reenter a dream. Saying softly to myself "Come on, come on, come on."

And he pushes the needle (a different needle?) down into my arm again.

And like two trains colliding, *all 142 passengers are presumed dead or buried alive in the wreckage,* I'm on my stomach and the arm wrapped around my face tastes like a gritty lemon paste, smells like orange bubble gum, like Circus Peanuts.

Light breaks open in my brain and shines on the back of my eyes, exposing broken vessels, tired retinas. Shock therapy in my arteries, buzzing like a blank radio and numb like a sleeping foot. I'm stuck here, roped and blocked with his fingers up my ass. No, wait, did I tell the fucking part already? How did I start this story?

Late at night, I drive out to the docks and stare out into the lake. And it feels like I'm drifting out, away from the shore, away from everything. I lie on my back, settle down in one of the concave places, rub my fingers against the wood. And the night gets so dark that I can't see anything. Even my hands, inches from my face.

And then I start falling asleep, but it feels different than this in-and-out stuff. I feel my body letting go. Uncontrolled, unconscious, uncomfortable. And no matter how hard I try, no matter how much I tug and grunt at the stupid ropes, I know that I'm about to go under.

And this beautiful creature with the tiny mustache, orange-scented forearms and perfectly drawn lips breaks open another bottle of clear something and stuffs the needle down into it. "Want another one?" he says.

I roll my head back, willing it all away, trying to scream into the void, but nothing comes out. All the hairs on my neck bolt upright, there's a continuous crackling of dendrites in my brain. I try to jerk away, and then—

Quiet.

I come out of it, shaken and unsure. The borders of the room materialize again, walls and windows and doors. And this grease monkey climbing up on top of me. And the hand is gone, the air sealed again, impermeable, like a see-through plastic surface.

And once more, the blazing white light of the needle going down into my skin.

My arms go limp, the rope slacks.

My eyelids atrophy, fail.

BREEDING SEASON

Taylor Siluwé

The sound of a close-by thunderclap rattled the room, drowning out the noise we were making.

Gasping for breath, my senses stabilizing, I rolled off him onto my back. My breathing slowed. I opened my eyes, and the elaborate glow-in-the-dark constellations on his ceiling came into focus, ever so slightly lit: Orion, the Big Dipper, all meticulously hand-painted during our brief season's interest in astrology.

Day had flipped to night. Thunder rolled again and a lightning flash lit the room as the sky exploded. Buckets of rain splashed down, splattering the windowsill. A few errant drops even reached my thigh.

I turned my head slowly, composing myself; a musky odor hung heavy in the air, his sweat was still on my tongue. He too had rolled over, and was staring at the ceiling, face flushed, hair rock-star wild. Purple passion marks painted his neck and shoulder, and red scratches marred his perfect pale torso, which rose and fell in quick gasps.

Globs of semen mingled with his dirty-blond pubes, glistened on the head of his dick and oozed off his thigh toward the carpet. White briefs and Levi's were tangled around his left ankle, held in place by one remaining Nike. He arched his back with a grunt, pulled a book from beneath him and flung it across the room. His arm collapsed to the carpet.

A tear trickled toward his ear.

Emotion swept through me, as dark as the clouds blotting out the light and as sweet as the breeze wafting over our afterglow, as gut-wrenching as the longing I'd harbored for two awesome years.

As I reached out to wipe that tear, I was whispering...*I love you.*

When we first met, I didn't understand his allure was sexual. Not right away. But looking back on the first day I set eyes on Ray—as he opened the door to his home in his tighty-whiteys, the only clothes he wore for the duration of my visit—I clearly wanted him from the start.

Unbeknownst to me, before I stepped through that door, before Malik had formally introduced us, before I got to see the killer fish I'd come to see, before I started following him around, mimicking his style in fashion and music and everything else, before all that, an invisible tether had sprung from my gut and Krazy-Glued itself to his scrawny, Fruit-of-the-Loom-clad ass.

His mother was vivacious and busty with sharp features and a pale toffee complexion. She was Jamaican, but her eyes indicated an Asian ancestor. When she was twenty-one she must have been exceptionally beautiful. His father was a mysterious Norwegian sailor Ray never talked about. His parents had met in Norway, and Ray was born there—exactly two months before me, but on the other side of the Atlantic.

I'd had almost every sort of pet imaginable by the time I was fifteen, the creepier and crawlier the better. I was just getting interested in fish when Malik told me about this kid that I should meet.

Ray's wild, platinum blond–haired head poked around the front door, his smile welcoming me like I was an old friend, ushering us in, even as Malik was making introductions.

"Ray...this is Danté. He's only got a goldfish."

My gut twisted into a painful knot and my right eye twitched. But with my left, I took in Ray's compact basket, a small scar on his right thigh, the translucent hairs on his arms and legs, and the fact that his pale toes were widely spaced. They reminded me of a gecko's. And he was a frail silvery-haired albino gecko—with the cutest accent—that I planned to take home and ask my mom if I could keep.

"C'mon, Danté." Ray grabbed me firmly by the arm. "Check this out."

We scampered down the long hallway to his room, which contained one huge aquarium and several smaller ones, all bubbling and humming softly. Tears for Fears' *Everybody Wants to Rule the World* blasted from his stereo.

Ray's two-hundred-gallon tank, dense with plants, was behind his bed like a living headboard, its black sand illuminated by a purple fluorescent glow. An explosion of misty bubbles rose from algae-covered miniature boulders, calling to mind undersea tectonic disturbances I'd seen on TV.

"Cool." That's all I could say.

I climbed on the bed with him. We knelt in front of his pride and joy, his hand on my shoulder, heavy and hot. I saw myself going home, picking up my five-gallon tank—with psychedelic gravel, pink plastic ferns and one lone goldfish—and hurling it out the window.

Once my eyes absorbed the initial spectacle, I noticed stout salmon-colored fish—with blue and green reflective scales adorning their sides like sequins—darting aggressively in and out of the rock formations, aquatic bejeweled gladiators tearing at each other, stirring up clouds of sand and then darting in opposite directions. Sometimes, they wouldn't clash at all, just face off, fins flexed, gills flared, growing redder and charging and backing up in unison, as if having a tug-o'-war with an imaginary rope.

"What are they?"

"Jewel Fish. They're always aggressive, but it's breeding season now, so it's all-out war. The male and female will fight and fight until she gives in and mates with him."

"Cool," I said again, cutting my eyes in his direction.

I forgot about Malik, who was probably in the kitchen raiding the refrigerator. I became totally engrossed in the action taking place on either side of the glass, as Ray and I chilled on his bed; him telling me all there was to know about breeding Jewels, me taking in every syllable, marveling that his hair was so silvery, his eyebrows so dark, and his hand so warm and moist.

It was a gray late September day when we played hooky and he broke into his mother's liquor cabinet. We were seniors at Snyder High by then, and felt entitled to take off whenever the mood struck.

It was about noon and we were gonna catch a movie—the premiere of *Dawn of the Dead*. It was supposed to be a real gore-fest, and I'd heard they did some really cool stuff with pig guts. We couldn't wait.

Ray came into the room, pale white-boy locks dangling past his shoulders. For the past year he'd been endlessly twisting them, trying to get his soft hair to lock. Achieving locks was difficult with his type of hair, but Ray wasn't one to give up easily. Actually, the job usually fell to me. He'd sit on the floor while I applied holding gel and methodically twisted each one. They'd begin to unravel the next day, and he'd call me over to his house to repeat the process.

His chestnut eyes sparkled with mischief as he waved a bottle, its clear contents swirling around and around.

"Jamaican Rum, one-fifty-one," he announced. "It'll fuck you up, so go easy."

I chugged straight from the bottle, then gagged and gasped. After Ray stopping laughing, he mixed some with soda and ice and we lounged on his bed, sipping our adolescent cocktails, watching his fish, flipping through copies of *GQ*, feeling worldly and grown.

One of his male Jewels was pummeling a female mercilessly because she wasn't ready to breed. She finally dashed behind the filter tube, pale fins shredded, chunks torn from her body. In the wild, she would be banished from his territory if she wouldn't breed. I knew that in a smaller tank with nowhere to run, he'd certainly kill her. I suggested Ray separate them, but he didn't believe in getting involved: survival of the fittest and all that.

"Breeding season is a beginning and an end," he'd once said in his sage way. "Why do you think salmon swim upstream to screw their brains out and die? It's nature's plan. And you shouldn't fuck with Mother Nature."

I knew that was true, but it still seemed cruel.

"Take my picture," he said, suddenly dropping a *GQ* on his bed and hopping up to get his Polaroid. "I'm gonna be on their cover soon. Mark my words." Then he struck a simmering pose and fixed a stare, and I knew he was telling the truth.

We drank some more while he posed and I clicked away. Soon images of Ray in sensual poses littered the bed. Then he took the camera, loaded more film and aimed it at me.

"Do something," he said.

I did. But he wasn't satisfied.

"Take off your shirt."

I did. He clicked again.

"Now do something sexy."

"Like what?"

"I don't know...lie on the bed and look at the camera like you wanna fuck it." Ray peered over the Polaroid with a smirk and a wink. "Or like you want *it* to fuck *you*."

An idiotic grin surfaced. But I climbed onto the bed and did as I was told, straining to erase my grin.

"I said *sexy*... C'mon, Danté, think about what really turns you on."

I gulped my drink, lounged back on his bed and allowed my thoughts to wander that secret passageway reserved for all things Ray.

There were memories, sensations, scents, and sounds from the two years I'd known him, drifting about in my head like those Polaroids on the bed, pleasure frozen in time.

The two of us in Exotic Aquatics, searching for some rare fish he insisted we acquire, the scent of aquarium water in my nose and an African Gray parrot shrieking "Fuck you" randomly... The two of us when I spent the night, lying in his bed, staring at the fish, talking about death-defying feats we wanted to do and all the little girls we wanted to screw... The two of us with the blanket over our heads in that same bed, masturbating in the dark, seeing who could finish first... Or the times we did it over the phone late at night, in our individual beds, racing to a hushed mind-blowing climax.

"Yeah. That's it." He clicked and clicked. "Now unzip your jeans. Show some pubes."

I was totally into it by then as he snapped picture after picture after picture, tossing them on the bed with the others, directing me to be more and more naughty.

"Roll over on your stomach. Stick your butt up. Think nasty thoughts."

Click.

"Yeah. Now pull your jeans down just a little...no, no...not like that, dammit. Let me do it."

He adjusted my jeans so a little crack of my ass was exposed, even making sure the white comforter was aesthetically rippled...and then told me to lick my lips.

Click.

He kept adjusting and arranging me. In no time at all, I was completely naked, lying on my stomach to hide exactly how into it I was.

Click.

Ray was more breathless than ever, circling the bed like a Mapplethorpe wannabe, biting his nails, in the zone.

"If you show these to anyone," I said to him, "you're so dead."

"Shut up." *Click.* "Arch your back." *Click.* "Do something else." *Click.*

"Like what?"

"Use your imagination for once. Damn, Danté, do I have to tell you everything? Just go wild."

I drained my drink. I looked at him, and excitement overwhelmed me. I started grinding my hips into his bed as I watched him watching me.

"Yeah. That's good. Just like that."

Click. He tossed the picture on the bed, scurried to a different part of the room, and aimed again.

I got more animated with my hips, adding lip and tongue action for effect, letting my imagination run wild...as instructed.

Click. Toss. Scurry. Aim.

"Yeah," he said.

I got on all fours, reached behind and played with my butt.

"Sexy. Keep going. Don't stop."

My finger slipped inside my asshole, involuntarily. I gasped. My eyes closed. I'd never done that before. Didn't know what made me do it then. The excitement of the moment, I guess. It felt nice though, extremely nice, exciting.

Then, as if some writhing sexual demon had swooped in and taken over my body, my shoulders dropped to the bed, my hips remained in the air, and my finger sank further inside. I wiggled and moaned with my face buried in Ray's comforter, enjoying this unique pheromone, and the sensations zipping from my toes to my scalp, but mostly, enjoying the fact that he was watching me...yeah...watching me.

Reaching beneath with my other hand, I began to masturbate, thinking of all the times we'd done it next to each other, there in his bed, knees touching accidentally-on-purpose during moments of frenzy.

My head lifted and I peeked through my lashes. Ray was standing there, camera lowered, staring.

I froze. I couldn't read his expression. It wasn't excitement or anger or disgust. It was just blank—like the observing eyes his fish must've seen as we watched them lovingly lay tiny amber eggs after beating each other bloody.

"Dude," he asked after what seemed like a millennium, "what are you thinking about?"

"You," I said, without thought, hesitation, or regret.

Ray nodded, put the camera carefully on the dresser, looked at me again in the same dispassionate way, and then slowly approached the bed. I closed my eyes because my hand was pumping again and he was coming closer and I couldn't believe we were finally about to do what everyone else, including my mother, feared we were doing.

Not that I was gay. But if I absolutely had to do some faggoty shit...I'd do it with Ray.

The bed rocked. He was climbing on. I waited, breathlessly anticipating his first real touch, one not casual or fraternal or accidentally-on-purpose.... I waited, already hearing his voice in my head as he knelt over me, whispering things, over and over, loving things in my ear in that cute little accent...and I waited for that first tickle of white-boy locks to touch my back.

"Put your clothes back on," he ordered.

My jeans landed on my back. I was lost in the fog of fantasy *interruptus*.

"Dude. You are *so* gay." He laughed. "I always suspected."

Kneeling nude on his bed with my finger up my butt, my lust immediately turned to indignation. Ray sometimes painted his fingernails black and wore eyeliner. He hated sports. He got pissed because I didn't know the difference between fuchsia and mauve. He'd also introduced me to the masturbating game...and he had the nerve to call *me* gay.

"What do you mean? You're the one who's gay!" I jumped off the bed and got in his face, my erection stabbing his belly button.

"Dude!" He stiff-armed me away. "Playing with yourself while thinking about another guy is the definition of gay. We won't even talk about that finger thing. Just put your clothes back on, all right?"

We faced off for a long minute, silently, Ray willing me to back off and get dressed, me willing him to come closer and get naked.

He broke the standoff. "Will you fuckin' get dressed, please? The movie...remember?"

I glanced at the photos on the bed, his, mine, all seductive, all leading up to the naked ones he'd urged me to do, and then I looked back at him and his smirk turned my indignation to something else.

"No!" A vein pulsed on my forehead.

"Dude. Please. Just get dressed."

"Not, not until you kiss me."

He laughed. "That's never gonna happen." He laughed some more. "I'm not the one who's a fag."

I pushed past his outstretched palms in a flash, pinning him against the wall, my forearm across his neck.

"Stop playin' around, Danté!" he gurgled, pawing at my arm.

"I'm not the one who's playing."

His shocked eyes stared back, filled with an emotion I couldn't put my finger on...fear, lust, anger, whatever... I don't know... I tried to kiss him but he turned away, yelling something I couldn't hear over my harsh breathing and beating heart.

But I could see his lips moving, shiny, wet, bits of spittle flying. It made me want to kiss him more, his shirtless, 501-clad frame writhing between my erection and the wall. By that point, I wasn't Danté anymore, and he wasn't my pale friend Ray with the cool-ass aquarium, silvery hair, and gecko toes. A sexual demon, a succubus, was in control now, making me do things...things I'd only dreamt about.

Ray's face turned red, which energized me further. I tore at the button-fly of his Levi's, slapping his hands away. We struggled further along the wall, dislodging photos, awards, a clock. A pole lamp crashed to the floor. We stumbled over it into the armoire, knocking books from the top and all sorts of crap out of the front. I managed to get his jeans to his knees, which finally tripped him up. We toppled to the carpet.

He tried to crawl away through the wreckage of his room, kicking at me, but that succubus was faster, stronger, smarter. Together we subdued him.

He exhaled, his body went limp, and he squeezed his eyes shut.

"Yeah, I love you, and I'm sorry." Ray's eyes were half open when I touched his face, wiping at that tear.

He slapped my hand away and then went limp again. But his jaw was tense, as if he was grinding his teeth, and a second tear oozed hotly along the path of its predecessor.

I felt sick. He was the last person I wanted to hurt, the last person I wanted to be angry with me. But he was, lying naked on the floor, wrestling with his emotions, trying not to cry, all because of me.

I reached out again because I ached to console him. I needed for him to not be angry with me. But before my hands could reach him—the same hands that moments ago muffled his screams—he sprang off the floor.

I sat up, watching him fumble with his clothes. His jeans and briefs were tangled around one sneaker. He methodically untwisted the material, angled everything appropriately, and then slipped his other leg back in and pulled them up. He pressed his palms to his thighs and slowly smoothed the wrinkles out.

I watched him slip into his other sneaker and carefully tie it up. Then, as he gathered the Polaroids from the bed into a pile, he stopped and stared into the tank at something floating.

His voice was far away. "Another one bites the dust."

He put the pictures in a drawer, stared in the mirror and tweaked his locks for a very long while, occasionally stopping to pose and flex his muscles, face dispassionate as before, eyes bloodshot.

His image began to quiver as moisture welled in my eyes. I felt overwhelmed and frantic, like all the oxygen had been sucked out of the air, like I was drowning in hot quicksand, like I was some tiny primordial thing sinking into the tar pits.

I closed my eyes and took a series of deep calming breaths, back to back....

"Dude!" he barked.

My eyes snapped open. I noticed the sun was shining brightly now, though rain still poured. Ray was watching me through the mirror with an expression that made my eyes burn.

"It's fuckin' late. The movie starts in forty-five fuckin' minutes. Get fuckin' dressed!"

I yanked myself off the floor, not as excited about pig guts and gore anymore, and did exactly as I was told.

FUNERAL CLOTHES

Tom Cardamone

Sung works at a little stall off Lafayette and Canal. They sell an abundance of T-shirts stuffed into a remarkably compact space; colorful stocking caps with the symbols of baseball teams hang, clothespinned to wires, from the low rippled-tin ceiling. Imperceptible until you are almost on him, a small old man sits in the tight corner, shaded beneath a broad visor, making keys behind a shelf of rolled shirts and the gold key chains of pocket-sized skylines. The visor obscures his face and, with his back to you all day, he appears to be fashioning something more than keys. Grinding away all day like that you would expect him to produce swords, something large and magnificent.

Sung, arms crossed, folds his tall body atop a stepladder in the middle of the sidewalk,

ostensibly because there's no room in the stall if even one customer enters, but also because this elevated position allows
him to survey the bustle for potential shoplifters. He does this
with a look of serious concentration; chain-smoking, perched
like a studious chess player, he sifts for crime. Since taking
the job he's only caught two shoplifters. A fat, tearful tourist
woman in a college sweatshirt tried to steal a key chain. He
caught her and blocked her way while shouting for police. Fel-
low venders poured in as her relatives calmly videotaped the
entire episode. And a black boy took a swipe at some hats.
Sung leapt from his perch to collar the kid, but an unseen con-
federate punched him in the mouth. He wore that swollen,
bloody lip proudly. When we kissed he would do so roughly,
pushing open the cut against my mouth, sticky warmth leaking out between us, painting the tip of my tongue red. After his
bottom lip healed he got it pierced, a silver ring that hung like
a handle, a doorknob I could turn but never open.

Besides key chains and lighters, he sells a variety of jade
Buddhas and fans and shiny, folded Chinese clothes.

"Only white people buy these," he told me with a huge,
knowing grin.

These were *Shou-yi*, funeral clothes, Sung explained. Dressing for corpses, for that prom the afterlife must surely be.
Surpluses, the odd sizes, off-patterns, were sold to tourists in
Chinatown, to white people, presumably as pajamas or Halloween costumes.

I come by at closing. My temp job in a midtown accounting office ends at five, so I kill time at the Strand bookstore or at Boy
Bar until seven. Sung doesn't like me to hang out while he's
working. I tell him he's not working, he's smoking. He answers

with a smile. Our apartment is close. Saying I live in SoHo sounds grand. It's not. Our room is half a living room divided by a sheet, fortified by a couch with a foldout bed, a white couch made beige from a variety of undefined stains merged into one dull color, like a cup of tea with milk gone cold. Our clothes have spun into piles in the corners, wrapped around empty cigarette cartons and old flyers for clubs come and gone and yellowed paper towels and crushed cans and empty beer bottles. Sung has at least one of every hat from work. They are strewn about like exhausted Christmas lights. He wears one every day all day, even while we sleep, when we fuck.

Sung fucks me with his shoulders back, his eyes shut tight, his prominent uneven front teeth pulling back his surging bottom lip, his stomach muscles stressed and sharp with crocodile folds. The grainy brown beads of his nipples are always hard. Alternating his hands behind his back and on his hips, he fucks me like he's doing tricks on a bike. I've finally been able to discern his birthday from the row of digits atop his passport photograph; he's two years older than he told me. We should start using condoms.

While he was at work I read his passport the way expatriates read foreign newspapers, looking for economic gossip from home. Facts that clarify, not straddle distances. In his passport photo he is wearing a fresh white Lacoste shirt, collar turned up. No cap. His hair is wild, not as long as it is now but definitely yearning to grow, stretching toward the edges of the photograph as if to pull the corners in, collapsing his picture in on itself. His passport photo dares shoplifters, police, the world to hit him, secretly knowing he'll relish the blow. Blood makes for better fingerprints. Malaysian-Chinese, Sung has been here on a tourist visa well past his allotted six months; two months ago he ran out of money and had to work. He left the youth hostel and moved in with me one week after we met.

The living room has no heat. In bed we pile on top of each other for warmth, spreading our coats over an old quilt our roommates begrudgingly lent us. As we change positions in the night I am always chasing his mouth, putting my lips near his. In the morning the room is heavy with the stale cream corn sweetness of his breath.

Part of the deal to rent out the living room is I can't use the kitchen. Since it's winter I keep milk on the fire escape. Cereal boxes are up on the bookshelf, all other meals we eat in Chinatown. At work I steal lunch out of the break room refrigerator, or buy a couple of hotdogs off the street. Part of the deal to keep this place is no television, no stereo. Sung lives with me though part of the deal is no one can stay over.

The couple we share the apartment with are students, musicians; they're extremely unhappy that we are in their living room, but the need to make rent doesn't give them an option. At first I tried to be friendly, but there is something anemic about this couple. They shy away from words, even to each other; most of their communication is a series of complex nods with their chins and a lot of pointing. Worse, they're one of those sad couples that have begun to look alike: they both have long, brittle blond hair that coats the tiny bathroom floor. Only the male's weak goatee allows me to tell them apart. Sung hates them and, as far as I can tell, has never spoken to them. He calls them Hansel and Gretel. At first I laughed, but now I frequently forget their names, lulled into their preferred form of communication when I see them: weary waves, nods, some pointing.

After work we go straight back to the apartment. Sung fucks me, hands on his hips. When he cums he exhales the sound of a collapsing church. I can't cum until I hear that sound, beams crashing down on me, lying across my chest. I shoot a river of frosting, pungent little wedding cake bells strung right up to my chin, and I open my eyes. Sung is looking at me, panting through an open smile, dry spittle whitening the corners of his mouth, the baroque musculature of his stomach brilliant with sweat. He looks at me the same way I examine his passport photo. Running his finger over points of departure, he smears the semen cooling on my chest in a circular pattern.

He hasn't said anything to me and I haven't told him I found the return ticket he purchased last week, hidden among his papers and passport; the date of departure, next Thursday, from JFK.

Snow on the roof spreads an alien topiary garden of crystal mysteries. We take the fire escape up here sometimes to smoke. In nothing but untied sneakers and cap (of course), wrapped in the dirty quilt, Sung sucks warmth from his cigarette, the cherry burning like Mars in a telescope. I took the time to dress and grab a coat. He finishes his cigarette before me and rushes down the fire escape and back through the window. I tap my ash out on the ledge, into the hole Sung made in the snow with his extinguished cigarette butt, hot ash melting snow to water, running off the roof in tiny black droplets. Part of the deal is that I not smoke in the apartment.

Tonight we'll go for dinner a few blocks east of Bowery, above Canal, a cheap Chinese diner. Imprisoned carp list to one side in the window aquariums, slowly blinking unfocused, molten eyes. Sung and I have a half-dozen restaurants where we can eat a full meal for five dollars or under. Afterward we have a similar number of East Village bars to drink in, but we always go to Boy Bar first. Friday nights I pick him up and we hit a check-cashing place on Elizabeth Street that has the best rates. We go to Boy Bar early to score. And here we divide. I like K, Ketamine. Sung likes coke.

It's the typical chorus line of hunched expectancy at the bar; we grab our usual booth in the back and order drinks, waiting. Everyone is waiting. In a sad synchronized swivel, every head at the bar turns in unison as the door opens. We always take the back booth, its leather seats held together by duct tape and desperation, to avoid joining the sorry expectancy at the bar. This has earned us a certain amount of favoritism from our dealer, Lonnie. Lonnie's going for a typical Lower East Side hipster look: rumpled, earth-toned clothes, faux–fallen rock star chic. He's always unshaven, a limp cigarette at the corner of his mouth, and though young his cheeks are jowly from constant drinking. The lines of his neck look dark, as if filled with dirt. He always wears a black knit cap low, right to his eyebrows. Often his eyes are secreted behind cheap, mirrored aviator glasses, the lens marred by huge, blurry fingerprints. He'll slide smoothly into our booth, waving over a drink, tipping the bartenders with a handshake laden with slim baggies of coke. This pays for his drinks and his right to do business here. We score over small talk. He treats us like friends, using our names way too often, in an unusually high voice. It's a forced, crackly casualness that over time has become authentic: the weight of paranoia that comes with his profession, subsumed by the singsong breeziness he's adopted to counteract nuanced fear.

He likes Sung more than me. He sits next to me so he can

look at Sung while he talks to us. Everyone likes Sung. He greets everyone by nodding his head and smiling. It's such a simplistic act of immediate approval I'm surprised it works so succinctly, so consistently. And his smile. His uneven teeth the opposite of ugly, Sung's smile is a roller coaster, a carnival billboard inviting everyone in for a good time. It gets free coke out of Lonnie. Or at least he'll front a bag or two before payday. After handshakes exchanging twenties and drugs, Lonnie takes his place in the bathroom, his roost between two sour urinals. The bar's patrons shuffle to the back, one after another, to score. He'll hang out in the bathroom for two hours, then leave. On the way out he always slaps me on the back. Passing the table he points his finger like a gun at Sung and makes like he's shooting him. Sung always laughs, grabs his chest and falls back into his seat. By now Sung has been able to do two or three bumps of coke off his wrist, so it's quite natural for him to show off the insane delight that is his smile.

I've done an equal number of rounds of Ketamine off my wrist, but where coke draws Sung's lips over his teeth and animates his eyes, K lures me inward.

Here kitty, kitty, kitty, kitty.

I love this drug.

I'll forget I've lit a cigarette and light another. Laughing, Sung will smoke my other cigarette without comment. Worse, I'll forget I've done a bump and do another. Forgetting that one, I'll do another. Once I went to the bathroom and forgot to come out. It was just so *nice* in there. Of course Sung didn't notice I was missing until he went to the bathroom to piss, and there I was, crouched on the wet floor, rolling a slimy, piss-soaked mothball I'd retrieved from one of the urinals between my fingers. Smiling away, I'm sure.

I didn't move here to erase myself. However, once K's smoky, marshmallow fungus began to converge on my memories, snuffing them out, I surrendered. It was like falling into a boiling parachute, the tentacles of its shredded tethers reaching out to pull me in.

I started smoking Marlboro Lights not because Sung did, but because I like the look of their cool stem, the gray-white smoke, new ingredients for my saltless soul.

This city is a picnic for sleepwalkers; everyone is together but completely separated, imprisoned in the library of his own particular dreamworld. This is a language of memory, one of images and places stitched together with bloody thread, thread stolen from the corpses of soldiers filling trenches with brown blood, so that your bedroom leads to your kindergarten class; the classroom's window looks out on an ocean of burning questions. No wonder the thread that bridges these incomparable places smells like kerosene. Or mothballs.

I need this drug.

I miss reading, though. I just can't seem to concentrate anymore. I'll sit on the train, a thick tome swiped from the Strand on my lap. The words make perfect sense, I mean, *I get it*. But I don't get very far. Fading away, I stare at the people on the train, weeding them until I only see the Asian boys, wishing earnestly the cute ones would stare back. And sometimes they do.

I used to have a ton of books at the apartment. They were a beer-rippled bridge to the past, proof I had gone to college: literary biographies, lives on paper about lives on paper. Pages that faded to white on the train. One day I came home from work and all of my books were gone. It was two days before payday and Sung had sold them so we would have money for dinner.

Another bump.

Sung does one, too.

I can tell from the way he's grinding his teeth that the coke has settled in the back of his throat, erosive and grainy. He gets up to get another drink. No. We're at another bar. Not sure I recognize this place. Everyone a frozen neon blur, and the music has really long pauses, like valleys, dark Columbian jungles gripping crashed planes, vine-wrapped skulls knocking against each other in the breeze, providing impetus for a renewal of beats. The song returns. I blink and everyone speeds up to normal. Sung returns with two drinks. Sliding one to me he asks, "You all right?"

I nod and wag the cigarette between my lips at him. He smiles and gives me a light. Smoking the last of a butt from the ashtray (another cigarette I abandoned?), he looks through the cloudy remnants, past me; I know he's gauging his internal clock. Time for another bump? He's trying to hold out for as long as possible, make the bag last all night. To fuck with him I do another huge bump, snorting it loudly, flagrantly, off my wrist. He only laughs and nods; cutting a presumptuous line on the table, he snorts blow through a rolled-up bill. I can't make out the denomination, though the dandruff-flaked president does wink at me, conspiratorially. I look around. Everyone is *alive*.

The next thing I know, we're outside a club in midtown, the Next Bardo. This was where we met. A knot of Asian boys in a variety of Armani Exchange knockoffs tightens by the door. It must be after midnight if there's a line to get in. Sung has left me smoking on the corner to see if he can get some old man to pay his cover. He'll go in with the guy, ditch him and then come back out, licking the stamp on the back of his hand to press it to mine, hoping that the resulting blurry, manufactured contusion will be close enough to the real thing to fool the astute Japanese girl working the door, sulking in a tattered boa. This is the plan and it's not working. Sung approaches every other old guy. The old men here are as cagey as they are desperate and intuit some kind of scam, waving him away. I'm bored and unsure of how we even got here. If we took a cab then half of our money for tonight is gone, wasted. Right now, I hate Sung. Taking these men by the arm, speaking in pleasing broken English when, having attended university in Australia, his diction is better than mine. Once he's escorting these old men, there's no reason to believe Sung will come back for me. He will leave me here.

Finally, a portly man consents to pay his cover. They go inside. I don't want to wait for disappointment so I walk away.

If the inconvenience of emotion is *this* present and rising then it must be time for another bump. Taking the train downtown, I go to another bar. Not Boy Bar. If Sung comes looking for me I don't want to be an easy find. I'm at a straight bar on Avenue B when I run into Lonnie. He laughs and feigns surprise when really his is a life where all surprise has long ago been drained away by rampant disenchantment and out-and-out lies. I mean, nothing surprises a drug dealer. But I get it and smile back. He's out of cigarettes and, ordering both of us drinks, hands me a ten, asking me to buy him a pack. Taking the bill I turn and pause, he smirks. We both know I'm going to do this and he's going to give me a bump.

In a bathroom stall we both smoke and take turns doing bumps off his wrist. He's doing blow, which I don't usually care for, it pulls me away from my K, drags me down the road of *now*, but I do it anyway.

Another bump off his wrist and as I lean in he puts his hand on the back of my head, gripping my hair.

I understand. Holding my nostril closed with one finger, inhaling coke, I feel a chemical heat sparkling up my nose. My other hand gropes Lonnie's crotch. Eyes closed, I breathe my last breath above sea level. Plunging down to my knees, I work his tan cock too quickly out from between the lacerating zipper of his dirty brown corduroys. I sense him wince but see his dick gain tumescence from the pain of the slight metal teeth.

"Suck it," he hisses.

Well duh, I think, putting him to my lips. I teethe at the bitter pout of his penis and feel his spreading flange across my tongue. Surprise. Lonnie coaxes a coke-coated finger into my mouth as well. Sparkle and numb. His cock rises as he gently shoves me further down, to deep-throat his cock. Loosening his pants, he pushes his underwear down to his knees; his bulging pubes scratch my tingling nose. I suck at Lonnie thickening in my mouth as if he were a source of oxygen, life. Everything I need. Disintegrating granules of cocaine bounce off my teeth as a slather of precum glazes my tongue. The bathroom tile is cold against my knees. I steady myself by grabbing his skinny ass with both hands. His buttocks contract in utter discomfort; Lonnie forcefully pushes my hands away.

I forget Lonnie's straight.

I pull away only to dive toward his balls. I gently tug at the loose, dank skin of his rubbery sac with my teeth, now pulling at my own hardening cock through my jeans. Lonnie expertly guides my mouth back onto his cock. He's ready. I swallow his bland load. My hard cock aches as I stand up, unsteady but awaiting my reward. He pulls up his pants. We exit the stall.

"Thanks, bro." Lonnie turns his back toward me and

strenuously washes his hands, like he's a surgeon having finished a particularly grizzly operation.

I just stand there, dazed. "Here you go." He hands me a fat bag glowing with K, telling me to let him go out first, and then wait a few minutes before leaving.

I nod, ready to go back into the stall and do a bump. He aims his finger at me and fires off a shot and winks, just like he does with Sung.

Wavering outside another bar, the cigarette between my fingers a long, bent icicle of ash. I'm busy erasing connections, first painting bridges white, then finding doors to lock, so I'm annoyed when Sung approaches. He's with a different old man than the one he went into Bardo with, and a really short, boyish-looking Japanese guy. Sung says something to me but I can't hear him. The Japanese guy looks at me like I'm a monster and draws closer to the old man; the old man is smashed, red-faced, smiling loosely with that ridiculous, benevolent grin certain types of drunks like to throw around.

Sung speaks to me. I see his mouth moving but I don't hear anything. The red starts to drip off the old man's cheeks, pooling at his feet like a fresh crime scene while the Japanese boy shrinks further, darkening like a crow at his shoulder.

I don't know what Sung is trying to say to me but I can tell it's *awful*. It's wrong. I swing at him. I want to put my fist in his mouth to stop the words. Desperately, I want to be the black boy that hit Sung. I always have. I miss him by what feels like a mile. The momentum of my swing spins me like a rubber corkscrew and I collapse on the sidewalk.

Sound returns. Sung's laughing, the Japanese boy is making whispering sounds in the old man's ear, the old man looks less red, more concerned, concerned I've stalled the oriental rotisserie of his sexual fantasies.

Reeling, stumbling, I tear away from him and rush toward Tompkins Square Park. The darkness suits me; the park clutches me and holds me to a bench. Collapsing, I pat my pockets for a pack of cigarettes. From where I'm sitting I see the old man hurriedly hail a cab. Holding the door he covetously ushers Sung and the Japanese crow into the backseat. I can't find my cigarettes. Looking around, no cops, I shake out another bump.

Death must be this bright. Morning light stabs at the corners of my eyes. I'm still on the bench. My neck hurts, my legs hurt. Dew has settled deep into my clothes, drawing the chilly dawn air to wrap around my bones. Blinking, I look around. A thin, weary woman with a small, black dog on a leash is staring at me. She looks away as I focus on her. No one else is around, it must still be early.

Light through waxy leaves, the pleasant sky is a yellow-blue. Piles of soiled snow slump beneath certain trees, hiding from the light.

It hurts to stand; really, really hurts. As pain spiders through my knees I try to remember last night. Nothing. A huge marshmallow. No, I remember Lonnie, looking down at me. No, his eyes are closed, but he *is* above me, like a daft puppeteer. And Sung. But for some reason he's red.

And Sung is striding down the street. When he sees me he waves vigorously and smiles. I blink. It's really him. He comes up to me looking fresh, showered, though still in the clothes he was wearing last night, so I know he hasn't been home.

At the diner again, dissolute carp hang in their overcast tanks. I seize my cup of tea between my hands for warmth. Sung orders soup. At his wrist a thick fold of twenties rests atop a fresh pack of Marlboros.

Sudden memory: we met at the Next Bardo. I wasn't even that high. It was late and I was confident I would score with someone. On stage Lucinda Williamsburg, a fat Filipino transvestite with a huge, quivering mouth like candy-glazed tire tracks, lip-synched Whitney Houston. I was staring at this Japanese boy with feathery eyebrows tucked into a Gucci hat. Baggy pants low on pointy hips; he kept his feet tightly together, to better accent new shoes, a pair of Campers that perfectly matched everything he was wearing. Sipping his drink through a pink straw, he was perfect. Just as he smiled in my direction Sung came up from behind me, putting his hand on my shoulder. I turned around and ran right into his gleaming smile.

Memories are abrasions, aging me.

The waiter brings us both soup. *Where did he get the money for that ticket?* I stare at the arrogant pleat of twenties on the table. I think about the date on his plane ticket. Every day it gets closer. *When are you going to tell me? Are you going to just leave?* He's always said he wanted to live in New York forever. *Just not with me.* I imagine him not telling me, just leaving. I'll meet him there, at the airport, dressed in funeral clothes.

I watch him lift the bowl, nose parting the steam from his soup. His nails are long, the dirt deep in their seams moist and clumpy, the fresh compost of nightlife; seeing this makes my heart spiral.

I'll rip the ticket up. I'll steal the ticket and go to Kuala

Lumpur, get a job in an American hotel gift shop, policing the aisles for shoplifters. No, Sung is in love with me. He knows our love can never be reconciled within his strict family, that his visa is expired. There is only one thing left to do. He'll immolate himself up on our roof, like those Buddhist monks did during the Vietnam War. The fire will melt all of the snow from the roof. People on the street think it is raining. Tourists stare up at the fiery glow while New Yorkers push past, obviously there's a movie being filmed. The ticket is meant for me. It's my movie. I am to solemnly deliver his ashes to his parents. Without a word I will hand over the urn, warm from my lap in the cab ride from the airport. My face made calm by a permanent sadness, a soldier in a war I resolutely believe in. I'll hand the ashes over to his father in the doorway, turning to leave without ever entering the house where Sung grew up. This single, direct movement will tell the father he has allowed his own familial shame to outweigh the very life of his only son.

The waiter comes to refill our tea. He is young, with black hair swept back like an oily, angry wave. I think I recognize him from the Next Bardo. He smiles at me, lingering at our table, filling my cup to the brim. I notice his pinkie fingernail is longer than his other nails, polished to a shine. When I lift the cup some of the hot tea is guaranteed to spill out onto my wrist. I smile back. Tomorrow I'll come back for lunch while Sung is at work.

FRANK FUDGEPACKER, TEENAGE WHORE

Simon Sheppard

I'm working my way through college, okay?

It's not my fault my cheap parents won't send me enough money, even though my dad's a professor and should fucking well know that college students have their needs. Man, he already gave me so much attitude about not being able to get into my top choices that I'm sure as shit not going to ask him for any more cash. But hell, I got to leave New Fucking Jersey and come to school in Florida, so what the hell, huh?

Oh, yeah…most of my clients call me Lance. Or Erik, depending. And sometimes, when I get all gothed up for the kinkier old men in my, um, clientele, I use the name Stiv. It's some old rock and roller's name, I think. One guy—he's not very nice, but he's rich as fuck—nicknamed me Frank Fudgepacker. You could call me Frank, I guess, but I'd rather you didn't.

So, yeah, I've always been attracted to older men. Sometimes *much* older men. I know, you'll probably say I have issues with my dad. Whatever. Listen, a guy likes to fuck what he likes to fuck. You, as a gay man, should sure as shit understand that.

When I was living at home, I didn't do anything about that. About wanting to have sex with old men. But when I got to college, I started sucking them off, sometimes. Men I picked up down by the beach, or at the mall. Guys who used to be married to women, or still were. Men who'd lost their boyfriends to you-know-what. Sometimes they'd be all nervous till I showed them my driver's license, that I really was eighteen. I know I look young for my age, but dude, it still seemed comic.

I'd usually end up back at their house, down on my knees, sucking. Some of them had real nice cocks, too. And even though they were pretty old—okay, sometimes *very* old—a bunch of them could get it up pretty well. Even without those little blue pills. As far as I knew.

They all seemed pretty pleased by their luck, too, even the ones who'd been nervous at first, thinking maybe I was a police decoy or something. As if.

Then I met Bruce. He was one of those AIDS widows, living on his inheritance in a pretty cool place, though it was a little pissy looking, if you know what I mean, all antiques and shit everywhere. Still, Bruce was nice. And I found him sexy, though mostly I like 'em hairier than him. Awesome cock, though. Thick, all veiny. And once he got his pants off, he did have hairy legs and a big bush. So.

I sure hadn't intended to have anything like an affair. I mean, I was busy enough just trying to keep up with math class. But I started seeing him kind of regularly. It was nice, really, and he started taking me out to dinner and stuff, even though I had to explain to him what "vegan" meant. I think he was happy to be seen with a guy as young and—well, fuck, I'll say it—as cute as me. No, I *know* he was happy. Proud, even.

Okay, once it got a little awkward when this straight couple, must have been in their seventies, came over to us and said hi to Bruce. I could tell he was trying to figure out what to do about me. He finally introduced me as a distant grandnephew. That was that. I doubt that the Steins or Cohens or whatever suspected a thing. I'm not even sure they knew what month it was. If you know what I mean.

Not that Bruce was a mercy fuck. Far from it. He was attractive. Wasn't even very old, just in his midfifties. And he was actually hella good in bed. He was the first guy ever to rim me. Until then, I had no fucking idea. How great it felt. No idea.

He'd get my legs up and scoot down there and start licking my hole. It was amazing. He was really, really good at it. Lots of men have done that to me since then, so I know. Bruce was really good.

He'd always said he loved how furry my crack was, even before he started slurping at it. Actually, my crack is one of the few hairy places on my body. Bummer, but there it is. I know…guys my age are supposed to all want to shave our bodies and be hairless as goddamn guppies. But fuck it. Guys my age aren't supposed to wind up in the sack with men old enough to be our fathers. Or grandfathers. Are we?

So he'd lick me and kiss me down there until it drove me

totally crazy. Then he'd raise his head up and I'd look down between my thighs—okay, back then, I could have stood losing a few pounds, which I eventually did—and there he'd be, his spit all over his beard and a big smile on his kind-of-handsome face. Then maybe he'd pull himself back up on the bed and lie on top of me, his stiff dick rubbing against my belly, his furry chest up against me, and he'd kiss me, a lot, and I could taste my ass on his mouth. Which was way hotter than it might sound.

Like I said, he wasn't a mercy fuck. He was a nice guy. Only I could tell he was pretty, well, romantic. Like he was always trying to avoid getting too affectionate, so he'd say stuff like, "Dave, I love...your hairy crack." Like he'd started out to say something else, but thought better of it. Which was smart, because when you're busy with classes, who wants some old guy to fall in love with you? Not me. But Bruce was nice, like I said, and not a mercy fuck. Actually, he was the first man ever to fuck me.

It had started out with him licking my asshole, as usual, then playing with it with his fingertips, just rubbing the wet flesh till I was fucking squirming.

"I want you to fuck me," I said.

"Really?" he said.

"Yeah, just take it slow."

"How about if I just lie back and you can lower yourself down on my dick? At your own pace."

"That'll work," I said. And it did.

Okay, well at first, when I looked down at his rubber-wrapped dick, I figured there was no way I'd be able to take it. That big thing was just not going to fit inside me. No way. But Bruce lubed me up real good and just let me slide down on it slow. And it maybe hurt a little to start with, but he played with my nipples—I like having my tits played with—and told me to relax, so I bent over and kissed him and just kinda slid on down, feeling that big old cock enter me, inch by inch, like I could almost measure it with my ass, I swear.

"I feel like I gotta take a shit."

"That's normal. Relax."

"I *am* relaxed."

"Relax more."

And that's when it began to feel fantastic. Anybody who says anal sex doesn't feel good has just never been fucked right.

So Bruce started to fuck me on a regular basis, sometimes twice a night, though school was actually getting kind of tough and sometimes I couldn't schedule in sex with him, or I had to stay up hella late studying, on the nights when I did end up getting fucked.

Bruce was always going on about how cute I was and how I was good sex, so I decided to take his word for it, and about then was the first time I sold my ass. I needed some extra money all of a sudden—some asshole had stolen my iPod and I hadn't even backed up most of the music. And my mom and dad were *not* going to be sympathetic about me being careless enough to let someone rip off my new iPod. At least not sympathetic enough to cut me a check.

It was easy to set up, really, the hustling. I put up an ad online, and after some emailing back and forth, this guy and I spoke by phone and he asked me whether I was a cop and I said no, I wasn't a cop, and yes, I had really just turned nineteen, and then he invited me over. He wasn't as good-looking as Bruce, but his house was a lot nicer—almost a damn mansion, really—and it was an easy two hundred bucks, since I probably would have let him suck my dick for free. Probably. Not that I ever would have told *him* that.

After that, I started picking up some much-needed funds, and it sure was easier than selling flat-screen TVs on weekends or asking, "You want fries with that?"

I was still seeing Bruce, though. And things had gotten a little kinkier. He'd even drunk my piss a couple of times, which was hot. Once I got over being pee-shy. Oh, he liked my foreskin, too. He was always going on about that. It's kind of long, see, even when I'm fully hard.

So one day during spring break, when I was still in my dorm room—because I didn't want to go north, and anyway, Florida is where everyone else *comes* for spring break—but my roommate was gone, Bruce came over, and we did some role-playing, like he's my professor and he's come to see me because my grades have gone to shit. But, he says, there's one way I can pass, and I ask him how, and he tells me that he really needs his dick sucked. Kinda hot, right?

I had his big old piece of meat shoved all the way down my throat when there was a knock on the dorm room door. We kind of froze, hoping it wasn't somebody from the college who had the passkey. Actually, at some point I started half-hoping it was my roommate Shawn coming back early, because he was actually pretty sexy, especially with his clothes off so I could see his big old dick and perfect ass, even though he was ostentatiously straight. Actually, though I mostly do go for considerably older guys, I'd every so often jacked off thinking of Shawn. That is, if I wasn't saving it for business. Thinking especially about spreading Shawn's cheeks and licking his hole the way Bruce liked to lick mine—maybe I'll be a good dirty old man someday. But anyway, after another knock or two, we heard footsteps going away down the hall, at which point Bruce started laughing pretty hard, which was kind of weird, seeing as how he still had his dick in my mouth. But that didn't stop him from coming...or from giving me a passing grade.

By that point, I'd built up a pretty steady clientele. I'd been seeing three or four regular johns every week or two, and there were also the one-timers who obtained my services when the missus was out of town or something. Most of them were pretty good guys, though one of them, a rabbi actually, could only come if he spanked me—I charged him extra for that— and another one kept offering me speed. I mean, he was old enough to be my grandfather and *he* kept offering *me* crystal. But mostly good guys. And there was also my damn school-work to keep up with, on top of business. So I started seeing Bruce less often. Taking rain checks on dates. Just blowing him off. Seeing him a lot less often.

But one night, pretty late, I was feeling kinda weirded out because a potential john had decided not to hire me, after I'd gone to all the trouble to go to his hotel room and shit. And he was pretty nasty about it, too, really, like what I was selling was somehow crap. So I phoned up Bruce, just to talk, y'know? And that's when I first told him I'd been hustling a bit. And he acted all nice and understanding—because, after all, he'd occasionally been fucking guys besides me, as well. Maybe he was glad I'd just been busy, and it wasn't that I didn't like him anymore, I don't know. Anyway, he was just so damn sweet that he managed to persuade me to head over to his place.

"Okay," I told him, "but no messing around. I'm beat."

But after we'd been lying around for a while on Bruce's bed, me talking, him trying to make me feel better, he leaned over and kissed me on the mouth, and pretty soon I had me a hard-on that was damn near peeking over the top of my jeans, and I knew that Bruce was going to fuck me, even if it was for the last time, and he did. And it felt great, no doubt about that. With experience, I've become relaxed enough to get boned any old which way: on my back, doggy, even standing up and leaning against a wall, which is what this skinny Mexican violinist who hires me likes to do. Still, I climbed up on Bruce and rode his cock, just like the first time, for old time's sake if nothing else. But then, while I was lying there with my head on his furry belly, smelling the drying cum, feeling safe and warm, he finally went ahead and said it: "I love you, you know."

And fuck, I didn't know what to say, so I said, "I love you, too."

And then he said, "I know." And pretty soon after that I got dressed and left.

So the weeks went by, and sometimes I answered Bruce's email and returned his phone messages, and sometimes I didn't. I mean, I was busy with studying for finals and I wanted to earn some extra cash so I can travel during the summer, when Florida becomes an oven with hurricanes. Plus, I really needed a new car, my old one was for shit. So we never got together after that night, the time I got turned down by a john.

Eventually, Bruce sent me an email that said, "I'm guessing that you don't want to see me again, but you just don't know how to say it. So I'll say it instead: Good-bye."

Well, though Bruce can be kind of a drama queen sometimes, the truth is that I was sort of relieved. It's not that I'd *never* have sex with him again, exactly, or that I want to hurt the guy. But what did he expect, really? I only have so much time and sexual energy, and business is business, y'know?

And also, here's something weird, it turned out that my roommate Shawn isn't really so straight after all. And hell, what's wrong with relating to someone my own age, somebody who won't die before I'm middle aged? I mean, sorry if it sounds cold, but it's true. So Shawn and I have started having this thing. I haven't told him about my work though, and I guess I never will, even though it's a bit of a job to keep it a secret from him. But he would never, ever be as cool about it as Bruce was. So I won't say anything about it, ever, and I hope he never finds out.

Bruce has called me a few more times recently, but I mean, what's the point? What's the fucking point? It's over, right? Not to be hurtful, but...unless he gives me cash...over.

And that's about it. That's the story. I know you said you didn't want to actually do anything, just beat off and talk. Oh, you wanted to do most of the talking? Sorry, sorry. But it's still the two hundred we talked about, right?

So you can finish up jacking off while I go piss, right? Hey, you want to come along and watch? No? You sure?

Okay, whatever you want, right?

Because, yeah, business is business.

Be right back.

CONFESSION ANGEL

Shane Allison

I remember, "Shane's got a boner, Shane's got
a boner!" I remember wrestling John Mattson
in the lobby of the movie theater where we
worked and desperately wanting him to fuck
me. He was heavy and musky on top of me. I
remember the jokes the boys at school made
about my wanting to suck their dicks, and with
some of them I secretly wanted to. I remember
Trent standing on top of a toilet while I sucked
him off. I remember puddles of cum on the
floor. I remember fucking myself with the handle of a spatula. I remember Lawrence Patter-
son's asscrack. I remember a tattoo of orange
and red flames on a dick. I remember jacking
off with hair, scalp and skin oil. I remember
kissing my friend Jack Lebowitz during a game
of Truth or Dare. I remember regretting that

I didn't dare him to show me his dick. I remember always choosing to tell the truth because I didn't want anyone to dare me to kiss a girl. I remember Daniel Stewart sucking me off in the bathroom of our junior high school. I remember the bathroom with its black and gold walls, the school colors. I remember his buck teeth. I remember him telling me that we couldn't mess around anymore because he had a girlfriend. I remember caressing Brian O'Connor's leg in social studies. I remember Dennis Miller having bad acne and pimples on his back. I remember the two Valentine's Day cards that Michael gave me that read, *Happy Valentine's Day, slut.* I remember eating that awful chocolate cake that accompanied the cards. I remember when he kissed me on the forehead. I remember being taken to the Hangar for the very first time. I remember that go-go boy smiling at me and feeling extremely special only to find that Michael was actually waving a dollar at him to dance for me. I was mortified as I stuck the money down into his Speedo. I remember grabbing Greg's ass as he stepped on the school bus. I couldn't help myself. He told everyone I was gay. I remember Brian Miller showing me his balls in math class. I remember when Eldridge James caught me jacking off in the bathroom. The entire school knew about it before lunch. For three years everyone called me "Jack." I remember the teacher's assistant that told me I had to go slow because he had not been fucked for a while. I remember my ninth grade phys ed coach. He had the cutest butt. I remember wondering what a jockstrap was and what it was used for. I still wonder about it. I remember needing to wear an extra pair of shorts under my sweatpants in gym so no one noticed my hard-on. It didn't work.

I remember filthy booths with cum on the walls. I remember Alan in an orange toilet stall. He was the first guy that ever tried to fuck me. The pain was excruciating. I remember jacking off to naked boys in *Freshman* magazine. I remember seeing a picture on Kirk Read's website of him licking someone's black motorcycle boot. I remember a poem called, "Eat Your Cum." I remember wondering what cum tasted like. I remember tasting my own.

I remember hot-pink dildos. I remember polishing my nails and trying on my mama's lipstick. I remember wanting to dress like a woman for Halloween. I remember hearing about drag queens duct-taping their dicks to their legs.

I remember picking pubic hair off my tongue. I remember the sensation of soft, limp dicks in my mouth. I remember the smell of musky balls at my nose. I remember a dick smelling like baby lotion. I remember a set of balls smelling like talcum powder. I remember the odor of unclean dicks, like shrimp or stale piss.

I remember gay personal ads in the *Tallahassee Democrat*.

I remember the buzz cut and how hot Jim Carrey looked in tight jeans in *Me, Myself and Irene*. I remember having hot fantasies about Bill Clinton coming on Monica Lewinsky's navy-blue dress. I remember wondering about the size of his dick, too. I still wonder about it.

I remember a guy asking after he blew me, how good his blow job was. He asked if it was in the top ten or the top five. I had to be honest and I told him it was in the top ten. I remember as I started to take my shirt off while this guy blew me, he said, "You don't need to be doing that."

I remember having a crush on Chris Mott after finding out that he was a slut. I remember all the jewelry he wore around his neck and on his wrists. I remember Nik dressed in black with long, brown, curly hair he used to wear in a ponytail. He wore lots of rings and had long fingernails like a vampire. I remember thinking if he were a vampire, I would totally let him drink my blood.

I remember the janitor with a Jheri curl warning me to stay out of the bathrooms or I would get in trouble. I remember the racist, redneck security guard who threatened to arrest me if I didn't stay out of the bathrooms. I remember looking through the slit of his stall at a guy picking lint out of his pubic hair. I remember a guy with curly hair, a glazed eye and a big dick. I remember his arm reaching over the wall of the stall at me. I remember the only two stalls with glory holes cut in the walls. I remember every stall being full. I remember *tap foot for blow job*. I remember a dick that was too big to fit through a glory hole. I remember a guy that kept saying, "Pull it, pull it."

I remember seeing a metal ring around a man's balls and trying to pull it off. I remember finding out later it was known as a cock ring. I remember big, blushing balls in a leather cock ring. I remember thinking that I had a foot fetish.

I remember when Ron told me not to shower before coming over to get my ass rimmed. I remember watching gay porn in Noel's room. I remember the copy of *Black Inches* he bought from a newsstand. I remember how tight his ass was in jeans. I remember how pissed I was when I found out he was dating someone seriously.

I remember cruising in the woods of Lost Lake. I remember a boy in blue swim trunks. I remember a man driving around in his car naked. I remember when he said he was *all sucked off*. I remember Sonny, who sucked me off on the hood of his Cadillac. I remember when he used to work at the gas station wearing his rainbow necklace. I remember seeing a guy walk stark naked through the woods like it was nothing at all.

I remember Collin giving me head in a park across the street from his house. I remember the cum stain I left on his brown pants. I remember how disgusted I felt after we fucked. I remember driving home with shit on my dick and a shit stain on the front of my underwear. I remember swearing that I would never fuck him again. I remember sloppy kisses in the front seat of his gray Mustang with the cranberry-colored seats. I remember making out with Collin in the back room of Panhandle Pet Supply where he worked. I remember the scratches on Collin's back as I fucked him on his couch. I remember his cat licking my scalp as Collin rode me. I remember thinking that Bisexual Cats would be a good name for a band. I remember shit on my dick again once I was done and not minding it so much. I remember swallowing Collin's cum and thinking afterward that he was not worthy of the privilege. I remember Collin standing butt-naked in the middle of his living room begging me to give him head (naïve bastard).

I remember the first time I swallowed someone's cum. I remember how I gagged. I remember how happy I was to find someone who was into eating ass. I remember when he said, "Give me that chocolate sauce," meaning my cum. I remember him sucking me off but stopping whenever he got email. I remember when he told me that he had a place but his wife was always home. I remember the noise we made as he rode me. I remember the beauty marks on his back. I remember how warm his asshole felt. I remember how pale his ass was. I remember pierced nipples. I remember big black boots with lots of buckles and realizing that he was one of those goth guys. I remember thinking *What in the hell have I gotten myself into?* I remember wondering why the walls of the sex arcade were being painted black.

I remember when the doctor at the clinic told me that I tested positive for herpes. I remember my cum oozing out gelatinously.

I remember Keerati, a cute boy I worked with at a computer lab. I remember looking over the stall and discovering how small his dick was. I remember a tiny hole in the wall of a stall, and written above it was, CHINESE GLORY HOLE. I remember thinking how rude that was.

I remember really salty cum and really sweet cum. I remember Brian's cum tasting quite sweet. I remember the cute Mexican with a really big dick he wouldn't let me suck. I remember a lot of men who were cock-teases. I remember a fat guy dressed all in black with a little dick. I remember a dick with lots of veins. It was gross and I refused to suck it. I remember really uncomfortable sex in my Ford Ranger with a theater major from Miami. I remember a man from Alabama with bad body odor. I remember an ugly Cuban guy with a really big dick. I remember the black-and-white photo given to me of a guy pissing in the woods. I remember gay porn magazines in sealed manila envelopes. I remember smokers' breath in my face. I remember dirty messages written in green ink on toilet paper. I remember looking at men's dicks while they pissed at urinals. I remember wandering eyes.

I remember wondering what George Michael wore when he was busted in that L.A. bathroom. I remember the impression soft dicks make through basketball shorts. I remember wondering how big Shaquille O'Neal's dick is.

I remember my first gay pride parade. I remember half-naked men on parade floats and Brazilian men in gorgeous black and yellow headdresses.

I remember when Chris said I have a nice personality and give good head. I remember running my fingers up the crack of his ass. I remember him holding on to my shoulders as he face-fucked me. I remember the blonde girls he brought home. He told me that one of them passed out while the other sucked his dick. I remember feeling pissed off and jealous. I remember riding to McDonald's in his PT Cruiser. I remember him telling me how good the McRib sandwich was, and trying it, but thinking that it wasn't all that good. I remember wanting to sit and talk with him all night, but he acted as if he couldn't stand to be around me another second. I remember when he told me I could come over to suck his dick because his girlfriend was at the movies. I was happy and excited. When I got there he told me that she had called and said she would be over in twenty minutes. I remember that Monday afternoon I gave him a blow job. I remember the black pajama bottoms he wore. I remember watching him through the window of his apartment. I remember his dick was so big he had to jack off with both hands. I remember the first two shirts I bought him from JC Penney. I remember us watching "MTV Jams" in his living room. I remember how happy he was before "she" moved in. I remember a bag of Hershey's Christmas Kisses and an ashtray filled with cigarettes. I remember notes on windshields. I remember giving him a heart-shaped chocolate wrapped in red foil. I remember when he came in my mouth and how bitter it tasted. I was going to spit it out but there wasn't anything around so I swallowed it. I remember how scared he was when he caught me standing outside of his apartment like a crazy person. I remember rushing home and calling to apologize. I remember being afraid that he would call the cops. I remember his hairy ass and wanting to give him a rim job. I remember, "Open your mouth. I want to shoot it in your mouth." I remember leaving because his dick was just too intense. I remember, "Come back. It feels so good." I remember when he wanted me to use my hand more. I remember, "Faster, suck me faster."

I remember Anthony who sucked me off in the parking lot of a library. I remember Jason who was only available on the first or second of July for sucking, getting sucked and getting fucked. I remember Dale who wanted to go clean his ass before getting fucked. I remember Richard and how his stomach growled as I blew him. I remember Von Ash in green shorts and a stocking cap. I remember making out on the floor in my bedroom and how his dick curled up like a hook. I remember when I wanted to stop having sex with him and how he begged me to continue. I remember pinching Greg's ass. I remember giving a letter to Thaddeus telling him how I felt about him. He hated me for it afterward. I remember meeting Matt for the first time. He wore all black with black boots and had a shaved head. I remember thinking that he was a white supremacist.

I remember the brown carpet in my aunt's bedroom. I remember the first time I jacked off. I was twelve, sitting on the carpet in front of her Zenith TV. I remember my cousin and other boys standing under a clothesline showing their dicks to one another. I remember kissing my cousin Darrin on the mouth while he slept. I remember seeing Jarret with his shirt off. He quickly put it back on when he saw me looking. I remember how Matt looked in his black leather jacket. I remember jacking off in the lower bunk below my roommate. I remember finding porn magazines in his desk. I remember attempting to fuck Greg, but he was too tall for me to get my dick up his ass.

I remember knowing so many men named John I began to think I would end up with a partner named John. I still believe that.

I remember jacking off with butter. I remember jacking off with mayonnaise. I remember jacking off with vegetable oil. I remember jacking off with syrup. I remember jacking off with toothpaste, but it burned. I remember not being able to come because I had too much to drink. I remember how pissed off I would be after waking up from a really hot sex dream. I remember the smell of egg custard during sex.

I remember a guy eating my ass, but stopping because he said it was too sweaty. I remember a guy rimming my ass and telling me that it tasted like shit. I remember the nineteen-year-old I sucked off. He wouldn't stop complimenting me on my blow jobs and said he would tell all his friends how good I was.

I remember Oscar, whose shirt looked like a picnic table-cloth. I remember making out with him outside of Stonewall Bar. I remember a guy walking past and saying, "Ah, true love." I remember walking into Christopher Street Bookstore, which really wasn't a bookstore at all, but a place that sold sex toys and videos and had a basement with booths. For ten bucks you could suck and fuck as many men as you wanted.

I remember jacking a guy off under the stall. As I followed

him out, he kept waving me away. When we got outside, his wife and kid were waiting.

I remember a man in Macon, Georgia telling me that his dick was only six inches. I remember peeking through a glory hole at a guy wearing panties and stockings. I remember a guy being thrown out of an adult video store for pissing in one of the booths in the back. I remember a man from Tennessee rimming my ass so good I came without him touching me. I remember getting my toes sucked and wondering why anyone would want to suck these crusty, calloused things. I remember finding a white pubic hair in my groin.

I remember calling the 1-900 numbers in the back of magazines. I remember lying about what they were when Mama saw a list of 1-900 numbers on the phone bill. I told her I was calling admissions offices of colleges out of town.

I remember jacking off to the drawings in *The New Joy of Gay Sex*.

I remember the first time I saw my daddy's dick. It was hung and uncircumcised. I remember using my daddy's tape measure to see how long my dick was.

I remember it all....

MINIMUM DAMAGE, MINIMUM PAIN

Jason Shults

One day Jimmy Dragon went crazy. He showed up at my apartment with a black eye and a loose front tooth, and when he stripped down I saw it wasn't only his face that had been hurt. He had hand-sized welts on his arms, chest and belly, and what looked like boot prints on his legs. I knew enough not to ask what had happened. When he fucked me that day, he told me to grab his ass, grab it hard and pull him in as far as he would go, leave marks on him if I wanted, scratches down his back.

"Hit me, goddammit," he said, his breath hot in my ear, his hands pulling my hands up to his chest. I tried to pull away, but didn't try very hard, even though I could have thrown him off me if I'd wanted to. My knuckles made weak slapping sounds against his skin.

"Hit me," he said, growling the words out. "Hit me."

I was on my back, my legs over his shoulders. Sweat was sprinkling down on me, dripping off the tip of Jimmy's nose, off his chin, falling to my lips, where I licked some of it up. Jimmy's humping made the rest of the sweat roll down the sides of my neck, tickling into my ears. Both of us were breathing heavy, gulping the apartment's stale air. Jimmy rose up on his haunches, shook his crew cut so that more droplets of sweat rained down on me. He let go of my wrists.

He grunted and said three or four words, what sounded like *something-something-blood,* and I was thinking, *Oh shit.* But I couldn't be sure if he was really saying what I thought he was saying.

Suddenly he stopped humping and, like a little monkey, flipped himself around so his ass was in my face. He grinned back at me with bared teeth. "You can't hit me, then at least get your fist in there. Right? You can do that, can't ya?"

I could. I could do anything for him except hurt him. I've always had a thing for him, always figured I'd do anything he asked. Something about his size, I think, not dick size because he's only pinky-finger big, but his body, I mean, him being so little you could carry him around in a backpack or a suitcase if you wanted. Maybe that's an exaggeration, but you get the idea. Back in high school he was just Jimmy Delano, one of those quiet kids sitting by himself in the back of the class, or in the corner of the cafeteria, not enough of a pain in the ass to make himself known, or to call down some bully's attention, just the quiet sort, reading *Star Trek* anthologies or the latest Frank Herbert, going unnoticed through his high school years. Maybe I was reading things into him that weren't there, but I always suspected there was more to the little guy than met the eye. And later, whenever he showed up at my apartment, whenever he said he wanted to fuck me, I told myself it was that sweet quiet old-time Jimmy I turned over for. I was fooling myself, but at least I knew it.

"That's it, big guy, keep going, keep going. Ah. Yeah. That's it."

I had about four fingers in there, working around. He'd never let me so much as touch his hole before, but I didn't ask questions. I tried never to ask any questions that Jimmy didn't want me to ask.

He leaned forward, knees and elbows on the mattress. He squirmed his ass at me, pushing against my hand, trying to get the whole thing in there. I finally got my thumb into the act, squeezing it in between my fingers, but then everything seemed to stop.

"Jimmy," I said, "I don't think—"

"It'll go, goddammit. It's going. It's going."

And suddenly I was inside him, up to the wrist, my arm poking out of his asshole like he'd just given birth to a twenty-year-old, six-foot-tall man, and the hand was the last to come out. Like I'd just been born, and Jimmy Delano was my creator.

"Holy shit," one of us said, but I couldn't tell you which one.

Our senior year, Jimmy had gone away for a while, disappeared, not noticed by anybody but me, probably. There was just a silent place, something empty, me wondering where he'd gone, wishing I'd had the chance to talk to him, get to know him.

When he came back two years later he'd already had the dragon tattooed across his back. I heard rumors about him before I saw him, that he was crazy now, that he'd walk up to anybody, peel his shirt off, and make sure they got a good look at the tattoo. Suddenly he was all about being around people, couldn't get enough of people, telling everybody, like some maniac carnival guy, "Step right up, take a look, take a look at this." He'd take off his shirt, turn around, and start talking.

The story changed every time he told it. He'd been in the Navy, he said, and got the tattoo in a shop in Bangkok. Or Fiji. Or he'd hiked across Europe and then Asia, ending up in Tibet, where he got the dragon during some kind of secret Buddhist ritual. Jimmy was smart, he'd read a lot, that much was obvious. But he couldn't keep his stories straight.

Fucking liar, everybody said, but not to his face. Most of the local guys, the few remainders of the old gang who were still in the neighborhood, turned and ran when they saw Jimmy coming their way. Couldn't take it, they said, telling me about it when they stopped at Koessler's, where I'd be sweeping up, cleaning the bathrooms, wiping down the tables. They'd shake their heads and laugh, "That Little Jimmy Dragon, what a fucking nutcase."

At first I couldn't figure out why he came to see me. I'd kept in touch with one or two people from school, but didn't hang out with them. I knew that Jimmy was back, but didn't have any reason to think he'd try to contact me. I was just biding my time, keeping to myself, telling myself I was trying to make the Big Decisions about my life. I did my bit at Koessler's, and jacked off when I got home every morning, pretending I'd get off my ass someday, apply to the local college, Be Somebody.

Then Jimmy showed up, out of the blue, knocked on my

door like some fucked-in-the-head Cupid had shot an arrow into his ass, and he just somehow knew I had its twin sticking out of mine. When I opened up, he came in, looked around a little, sat down on my filthy old couch like he owned the place. His foot jounced on the floor like he had something to say, but couldn't decide whether or not to say it, so he didn't say much of anything. Finally he said *Hey*, and then he looked around some more. When I asked, he said *Nah*, he didn't want anything to drink, just wanted to see where I lived. A few minutes later, he stood up like he was ready to leave, but then he came over to me, pulled his T-shirt off over his head, turned around so that I could see the dragon on his back. I'd heard about it before, of course, but it was the first time I'd seen it.

"Go on," Jimmy said, quiet, his voice an octave too low. "Touch it."

I touched it.

"You'll never guess how I got this motherfucker."

I don't think it was really the sex he was after. Some people say sex is the answer to everything, but it seems to me like that's too simple an answer. Sex is never just sex. Mostly Jimmy came to my place to try out the new stories, I think, since I never questioned him, never let on that he'd told the story before, or that he'd said something completely different last time. And I was horny and I guess lonely, and wanted a little human contact, and my crush on Jimmy hadn't gone away, never did go away, even after I found out about the lies. I think Jimmy fed on that need, my need, satisfying needs of his own that weren't just about getting his rocks off.

He'd put on some weight while he'd been gone, muscle weight, not much but just enough to show the veins in his biceps and the ones running down by his hip bones, blue-green veins worming up over the washboards, held down tight by his light brown skin. He liked it when I traced them, my fingers running along his arms, his shoulders; down his belly to the insides of his thighs. He wouldn't put it into words, or ask me outright to do it, but Jimmy liked it when I touched him slowly. He liked to be...adored.

He came around more and more, started telling me about his family. From Puerto Rico, he said. Or Cuba. Or Venezuela. He told me his sister had had her head cut off by a sugar cane harvesting machine. He told me his little brother died from asthma in the Andes. His parents had been killed by rebels, or had died of diphtheria in some jungle.

Whenever Jimmy climaxed, it was like an explosion going off somewhere inside his brain. You could see it on his face, a thousand different expressions fighting for a place there. The first time I saw it, I thought he might be having an attack of some kind. I didn't know him very well then—not that I ever got to know him very well—and I thought maybe he had epilepsy, or maybe he was having a stroke or a heart attack. He seemed to pull away from me completely, going somewhere all his own. His eyes shut tight, his mouth gaped open, looking like it wanted to yell something, but I guess I blinked and then he seemed to be smiling, peaceful, and I blinked again and then his thin eyebrows lifted up, questioning something, his eyes still closed. All this happened in the space of a few seconds, the time it took him to pump out a few squirts of cum. There's more that happened, too, that face, but it's not like I can put it into words. It just seemed like Jimmy took a trip when he came, maybe his life flashed before his eyes, or maybe he was on a planet somewhere where time happened a lot faster than it happened here. Maybe he was living a whole lifetime on that planet, just in the space of a few seconds, or maybe he was making a list, just that quick, of all his hopes and dreams and regrets and joys or whatever of his real life here on earth, adding them up, trying to figure it all out.

I couldn't say for sure. I just know it scared me a little, every time.

Jimmy'd flipped around again, facing me, was bouncing up and down on my cock, but then suddenly he stopped moving. I could feel him loosening up. Not his ass I mean, which was about as loose as it could get, but just his body in general, his tight little muscles going slack. He leaned down close to me, close enough I thought he might kiss me, but at the last minute his body twisted and he rolled off, climbed off the bed, and marched across the bare concrete floor of my bedroom.

He'd done this before, climbed off in the middle of the ride, leaving me feeling empty, cold, sticky; now he had left me feeling suddenly alone, lonely, while he went to fetch his bag. He carried an old army surplus knapsack with him everywhere, not something you'd see the troops carrying these days, but an older thing, Vietnam or Korea era, a thin canvas thing, olive drab, worn and frayed by years of use. I don't think Jimmy really thought people would believe he'd carried it in combat but it did give him a slightly military look, gave the impression that he'd been through something, been through a lot of something. At least to me it did. Like I said, I was pretty young back then.

But the bag he went to get wasn't the knapsack. It was a bag within the knapsack, a small leather pouch, black and shiny, newish, hand wide, the top zippered and sloping, making the whole thing almost triangular. It never occurred to me what the bag was actually made to hold. I knew that Jimmy kept his stash in there, sometimes prerolled, sometimes loose but with a pipe. Sometimes it was a toy or two, something he wanted to try. It'd been seven months since we first started fucking, and I could tell that Jimmy was bored after the first couple of times. After that, one by one, came dildos, poppers, handcuffs. Once he had a thong in there, leopard-spotted, that he asked me to wear around the apartment, "just walk around, regular-like, like I'm not even here," while he drank a sixpack of Old Milwaukee on the couch. Afterward he didn't even touch me, just grunted and nodded and walked out the door. A few days later he was back, without the thong but with the pot, and he fucked me even if he didn't want me, him blissed out, counting the tiles in the ceiling, with me doing all the work; fucked me because I was available, because I was willing.

A few days later he asked me to tie him up, burn him with a cigarette. Just around the nipples, he said, maybe a couple on the inner thigh. It was early enough in our relationship that the fire or whatever between us was hot enough, I was feeling I guess vulnerable enough, that I couldn't say no.

When he came back from the living room, he didn't even try to hide the gun. I didn't know anything about guns back then, but now I'd guess it was a .38 police special Smith & Wesson, silver, shiny. It dangled at his side, carried casually in a limp arm. I noticed his dick, too, limp, withered up like it wanted to crawl back inside him.

I sat up on the bed. "What the fuck, Jimmy!"

"It's okay," he said. He sat down beside me, set the gun on

his naked brown lap. A bruise on his left thigh was purple, turning black. He had another bruise on the back of his right hand, the same hand that was spread out gently over the gun. "I was just wondering if you'd do me a favor, that's all."

My mind ran through about a million different scenarios. The only one that made sense was that Jimmy had found the gun, or stolen it, and he wanted me to keep it for him. I don't think I really knew my limits back then, not so that I could rationalize them, think them through to myself and know for sure what I'd do or wouldn't do, but I knew without having to think about it that I wasn't keeping a gun in my apartment. I shook my head, started to say as much, but Jimmy stopped me.

"Just a quick shot through the shoulder," he said. "I heard that's the best way. Might mess up my arm for a while, but it heals quickest and won't hit anything too vital. You know?"

"Oh, for fuck's sake—"

"No, really," he said. "It's not a big deal. I read up on it. Through the shoulder. Minimum damage, minimum pain. Afterward I head down the street, call an ambulance from some pay phone." He looked me in the eye, something he didn't often do. "Don't worry. I won't tell anybody how it happened."

"People will hear it, Jimmy. The neighbors."

He laughed. "In this building? In this neighborhood? Nobody'd even call the cops."

I sank a little, defeated. Jimmy was probably right. There were two crack houses on the block, and right in my own building there were three rooms on the top floor reserved by a pimp I never saw but whose girls sashayed up and down the stairwell all night long. One of the girls had overdosed the previous month, leaving a vomit stain on the hallway carpet, probably the only mark she'd made in life. A few weeks before that, one of the johns had been beaten to death with a tire iron. In a strange way, I'd started to consider it all normal, take it in stride. I'd stopped calling 9-1-1 after the first couple of times I heard gunshots because, the times I'd called, the cops hadn't shown up for hours. Sure, Jimmy was right. Nobody would care, nobody would call.

But in the time it took to understand this, I understood a lot more, too. I could figure out Jimmy's motivation easily enough—to him, the gunshot was just another version of the dragon tattoo—and I knew he was smart enough that he'd probably been using me for a long time, building up trust, trying to get to this very point. I was thinking, that's what the handcuffs were about, the fisting, the cigarette burns. And, no, it wasn't about the sex, at least not entirely. In the space of about a minute, I had a hundred sudden revelations like that, and one of those was the fact that I couldn't see Jimmy anymore. This was the end of it, one way or the other. I knew I couldn't do what he'd asked.

He saw it in my face, I think. His body made a move like he wanted to argue his point some more, but he didn't say anything. He stood up from the bed, went to the living room. Shadows on the bedroom wall told me he was getting dressed, packing the gun away. He opened the door and left.

This is the part where I'm supposed to tell how I saw Jimmy sometime later, showing off his gunshot wound to all the boys at Koessler's. How he'd gained their respect because he'd finally proved that he was a real man. He'd be telling a story about how he got it. Maybe he'd finally get the story straight this time. Moral: Jimmy Dragon had learned his lesson. Or maybe the guys would laugh at him because he'd given three different versions. Moral: people never change.

Or then there's the tender ending: I tell how he came back to me after he'd found somebody to give him that shoulder wound, and how he couldn't make it to the hospital, and he was full of regrets about trying to be a show-off, and he died right there in my apartment, in my arms, with me giving him whatever absolution I could. And then I cried or whatever, washing away his sins with my tears. Moral: everybody needs forgiveness, redemption, love.

But that's not what happened.

Long story short, I never heard from Jimmy again. He left like he had in high school. I never heard his name mentioned. The guys at Koessler's forgot him right away. I thought about him sometimes, mostly at the beginning, right after he'd gone. I wondered if he'd accomplished whatever it was he wanted to accomplish. I doubted it. From time to time, after that, something would remind me, and I'd stop and think about him. I'd be reading in the paper that some Tibetan monk was making a once-in-a-lifetime visit to our city, and I'd think, *Where's Jimmy?* Or I'd hear about a farming accident, where somebody got an arm cut off by a threshing machine, and there it would be, the thought: *Whatever happened to that guy I used to know? Right, that one with the tattoo?*

But every now and then, late at night, when I'm alone and lonely, it all comes back. Every bit of it. And sometimes I feel like writing it all down, trying to dredge up every detail before this memory blurs into something else.

RELEASE

Alana Noël Voth

I met Asa at a volleyball game on a beach in
Newport, Oregon. The rain was crazy that
day and the players were up against the rain
as well as each other. I didn't like volleyball; I
liked to look at the guys. Four on each side of
the net, cords of muscle in their arms and legs,
clenched buttcheeks, and wet hair.

One guy served the ball and sent it into flight;
for a second the ball dangled like a moon on
a mobile, and then it struck the ground, and a
second guy grabbed the ball, cradling it to his
chest. The guy who'd served hit the ground
on his stomach. When he stood, wet sand
stuck to him like bruises, which he brushed
off, smiling.

I'd had a few beers before hitting the beach.
The cigarette I tried to light was a limp dick, so

I returned the pack to my jeans pocket. Camel Lights, same as Dad. I started smoking when I was ten. I hadn't worn a shirt to the beach; I was pretty skinny.

"You're cold," a voice said behind me.

"I'm fine," I answered without looking over my shoulder.

"But you're shaking," the voice spoke again.

"It's nothing." This time I looked. If he hadn't been cute I would have blown the guy off. He looked my age, twenty-seven, medium tall and slim but not bone-skinny. A hooded jacket framed his face. Green eyes. Lashes so thick you would have thought he wore mascara. Bangs stuck from under his hood, hair the color of raisins. I ate raisins as a kid. Sometimes they were all I ate.

"You like volleyball?"

"I like rain," he said.

"Well, the shit likes you too." I wiped my face with my hands. "You're not from around here, are you?"

"Arizona."

"Shit. What are you doing here?"

"You know the aquarium?"

"Yeah, huge tourist trap."

"I've got a one-year grant from school."

"For what?"

"I study seabirds."

"That's weird, in a cool way," I said.

"What's your name?"

"Damon."

"Asa."

"You've also got a weird name, Asa, but it's cool." I shook water out of my hair. "I've got to get out of this shit."

"Want to go?"

"I've always wanted to see Germany." I was being a smart-ass.

Asa laughed.

"Seriously, German guys, totally scary."

"What are you talking about, isn't that a little World War II?"

"My dad's German, and he's a prick."

We both got quiet. Waves came in, closer and closer to our feet. The guys playing volleyball had given up. The ball was abandoned on the beach, scabbed by sand. The players slapped each other on the back, and they smiled even though their game was ruined.

"My place is four blocks away," Asa said. "It'd be nice not to hang out alone all day."

Actually, I planned on heading back to a house where I crashed with some jerks from a bar. I thought I'd jerk off to some gay porn. Once in a while, I came across a film I'd done, and I'd stare at the screen thinking, *When did I do that?* Then I'd beat off focused on the other guy's reaction to my cock up his ass, his mouth on my meat. How he liked me so much.

"I've got a warm shirt, a few beers, and a TV," Asa said.

His offer was generous, so I figured I knew what he wanted.

Asa's apartment was simple, living room, kitchen, one bedroom, and a bathroom with a tub and shower. In the living room, he had a sectional couch and a big-screen TV. Imagine watching porn on that. I'd never seen so many damned birds in my whole life. The entire place was covered with them: sketches of birds signed with Asa's name, pictures of birds from magazines, posters of birds in flight, bird diagrams and bird skeletons—which kind of gave me the creeps. So delicate thin you could crush their bones with your bare hands.

"So why don't you have any pet birds?" I asked.

"Don't want to keep birds in cages."

"But you work at the aquarium."

"For conservation purposes, yeah."

I sat on the couch. Asa had given me a shirt, but I hadn't put it on. My nipples were hard. "Come here," I said.

Asa sat beside me. "Hungry? I could make chicken with rice."

"You eat birds?"

He laughed.

"What's so funny?" I grabbed him by the back of his head, then kissed him. Asa pulled away. My dick was killing me. "C'mon, let's make out." I kissed him again. Then I grabbed his hand and put it on my crotch. "Jerk me off, then I'll do you." I moved my hips, pressing my cock against his hand. I was nervous around him, and so sex was how I'd decided to handle the situation. We'd get off. He'd like me. That was how it worked. I knew what he wanted.

Asa moved his hand to my stomach and then rubbed my skin there in circles. I stuck my tongue through my lips before I sucked in a breath. "That's nice." It was. I slid my hand over his crotch. He was hard. After a minute he pushed my hand away and then curled one of his around my hip. I waited. He scooted closer then leaned his head in the space between my neck and shoulder.

"What are you doing?" I couldn't relax.

Asa put both his arms around me.

A month later, I moved in. Asa had caught on to my living situation, that I crashed with some jerks from the bar, and said,

"You can't do that. I'll worry about you." Sweet enough, if not slightly suspicious, but after three dates, I guess you could call them, Asa had let me jerk him off, and then he'd done me, and then I'd sucked him off one day after that, and he'd just about gone nuts while I worked on him. "Jesus…Christ… god…Damon," and when I'd finished, proud of myself, mouth full of jizz, he'd given me this look I took for supreme lust, what else, and then he'd said something like, "I don't want anything to happen to you," and then I moved in here with a bag of clothes and a bunch of CDs, mostly goth, angry aggressive stuff like Sisters of Mercy and Ministry.

"This is horrible crap," Asa said the first time I played him a CD, and I'd let my eyes bulge like *Are you crazy?* What did he listen to? Some truly sappy sick stuff: Gordon Lightfoot, Carly Simon, Jim Croce, Barry Manilow, and Carole King.

"We're like oil and syrup," Asa had said.

Sometimes Asa was…very abstract. Like a poet or something. I wasn't used to it, but I stuck around because I was curious or because I was better off here than where I had been before. Anyway, we got into a routine. Asa spent his days at the aquarium, and sometimes I stayed in the apartment and cleaned it; I even tried to cook but then I burnt some oatmeal and gave up. Other days, I went to the coffee shop and smiled enough to earn tips then came back and put it all on the table for Asa, except what I kept for cigarettes. When Asa came home he took a shower and then cooked us a meal. He was probably the best cook in the world. He made stuff like Ethiopian chicken, sweet and sour shrimp, and lobster linguine. Stuff I'd never had before, and so I started to put on some weight. After dinner, Asa sat beside me on the couch and read ornithology books, which was a big word for studying birds.

Asa would tell me stuff: some birds ate red meat; some birds nested the same place every year; in some birds, the guy was better looking than the girl; some birds migrated; some mated for life. Then Asa told me about holding a bird in his hand while it died.

"You don't hear or even feel it so much as you experience a sense of leaving," he said. Then Asa shook his head. "I can't explain it, exactly, but the experience comforted me, maybe because it was peaceful, and I constantly worry death is violent, like all this thrashing around when in fact it's just a flutter."

I looked at Asa then and felt afraid. I mean, what do you say? And how do you keep the relationship at a safe detached distance when the other guy *says* something like that? Basically, I changed the subject. Luckily, a horror film was on TV, and so I pointed out a birdlike man-creature tormenting a bunch of teenaged boys on the screen.

"Why do you like movies like this?" Asa asked.

I shrugged. "Been watching them since I was a kid."

"Your dad let you?"

I didn't look at him now.

"Let's talk about your dad," Asa said.

"No. I'm not talking about my motherfucking dad. Forget it." Then I looked at him, and Asa watched me, which made me suddenly paranoid he saw too much. "Let's fuck," I said as a distraction, anything to get away from the dangerous stuff like talking or getting emotional. Sex was my safety net, familiar territory, something I was good at—fucking, making people happy that way.

"C'mon," I said. "You want to." I lifted my shirt over my head, tossed it aside and stood before him. Asa liked to look at my body. He'd tried to sketch me once. I touched my ribs, drew circles around my nipples until they got hard. "I'm horny for you. See?" I kicked off my jeans, then my boxer shorts, and then showed him my cock, stroked it, pushed the skin up and down to work out some pre-come, and then I got a little come on my finger and ate it. "C'mon, baby. I want to fuck you." I sounded awesome, like a porn star. "What do you say, huh, let me fuck you, yeah? I love your ass."

Asa watched me from his chair. "You love my ass?"

"Uh-huh." No more words. I went to my knees on the floor. When I reached him I cupped the shape of his knees through his pants then pushed his legs apart and rubbed him through the denim.

Asa leaned forward and pinched one of my nipples; the sensation was sharp as a gasoline smell. "Fuck," I said.

Asa kissed me on my mouth. I kissed back. Then with my fingers fumbling, I opened his pants and got his cock out. He sat back and watched me. I fit his cock in my mouth, then let it bump the back of my throat and then fill each of my cheeks like an enormous gumball. I worked on his cock until he was about to come, which I knew by the spasm in the corner of his mouth, so I stopped.

"Damon," he said. "Jesus Christ."

I motioned him down. Asa lowered himself to his knees in front of me then dragged his hand through my hair to my face.

"Look at me,' he said.

I put my hands on his hips to turn him.

"Look at me, in my eyes."

I looked and saw a feather in Asa's hair. I was surprised to see it and fixated on it. It was kind of funny. Asa grabbed my face. We wrestled. I got my arms loose and pinched the feather from his hair and then showed it to him. Asa sighed. I pressed the feather into a ball between my fingers. Then holding Asa by the hips I turned him. He shifted without a word then leaned forward over the chair, putting his ass in perfect position. I oiled my cock with spit then pushed the head at his asshole. He opened a little at a time for me. Soon I was all the way in and moving. I had this thought his ass was moist and sticky as fish gut. I sank further, sandwiching him between me and the chair. He moaned underneath me.

I could talk again. "Feels good doesn't it?" I fucked him. "Yeah, it feels good." The base of my cock felt wedged at the mouth of a channel, but beyond that, open sea. "I'm going to come up your ass, babe." Then I did it: I dug my nails in his hips and shot off. Asa breathed heavy, and I stayed inside him and reached around and found his cock. Together we jerked him off, up and down, around to his balls, up to the head. I felt him pulling air into his lungs.

"Want me flat on my back?" I asked. "Want me to throw my legs over my head and open my asscrack up? Want to fuck me like that?"

Asa moved our hands faster. The muscles in his arm flexed, and then he gasped, and a ribbon of spunk splashed my hand. He took hold of my wrist. "What if I fall in love with you?" he said, trying to see me over his shoulder.

My cock slipped from his ass then, and I crawled backward. "Hey, it's just the sex talking, babe, because it felt good, that's all."

When Asa slept he frowned, like something that didn't bug him during the day rushed him at night, then ransacked him. He made sounds in his sleep, which woke me and then left me sitting on the bed inside a yellow stain of lamplight. I watched him sleep.

I didn't sleep well anyway. I'd suffered years of insomnia. After a while you got used to a punch in your stomach waking you up while you slept with a pillow over your head. "Get up, join the fucking party." Dad roughed me up as a way to entertain his friends. He'd hit me up the side of the head, give me a shove. He made me wait on his guests, clean up after them and say things like, "I'm not a pussy." Dad liked everything rough—parties, poker, people. His girlfriends always looked like hardened plastic. One used to come to my room and suck my dick. She'd say, "Your dad shouldn't talk to you like that; you ain't no pussy." I couldn't help it: I shot off in the woman's mouth making believe she wasn't a woman, not a woman sneaking into my room, or a woman Dad fucked and beat up.

I wanted to know what or who ransacked Asa's sleep and I scooted close to him on the bed at night and tried to read the lines in his forehead like a palm reader would read your hand. I couldn't see anything, and then he'd make a sound, as if he strained against the sheets, and I got so close I nudged him.

Asa opened his eyes. I scooted away, and then he focused his gaze on me. "What is it?"

"Nothing. Sorry if I woke you. I must have, you know, jostled the bed, sorry." I wondered if he knew I'd been staring at him while he slept.

"It's okay." Asa yawned. "I had a dream, I think."

"About what?" I really wanted to know without showing I wanted to know.

"It was weird, like I was stuck and couldn't move."

"I've had dreams like that before. I want to run but can't.

Was something chasing you?"

Asa thought and then shook his head. "My mother drowned, for real I mean, not a dream."

I nodded, trying not to blink. Short spasm under his left eye.

"I was there," he added and then rolled over. I realized I was supposed to comfort him, that a lover would do that, but I sat on the bed instead fixing my eyes on the back of Asa's head like a kid frozen to the side of a pool while his mother drowned in front of him.

Not long after that Asa brought up the worst idea in the world.

"I met a guy, nice guy, who's a therapist, and I thought you could talk to him."

"What? No. I'm not talking to a shrink."

"But if you can't talk to me about your dad, I thought you'd talk to him."

"No. I mean it, just drop it." I stood from the couch, walked across the room and then felt like the ball those guys on the beach had hit back and forth a few months ago; I paced the room.

"I thought I might talk to him too," Asa said.

"Whatever, if that's what you want."

"But I think it would be good for both of us, you know, to deal with our crap."

"You knew what I was about when you invited me here," I retorted. I was mad and decided I had to do something. What I did was throw a beer I had in my hand, which hit the wall with a thump. Asa didn't move. Usually if I did that, a guy hit me.

He said, "Damon, I just want to talk."

I was out the door.

Not much later, I sat inside a bar. I wasn't sure how many drinks I'd had, but I smoked at least twelve cigarettes, and my heart felt like it was striking the bars of my rib cage and wanted to get out. One of the jerks I used to crash with showed up and sat next to me. Cole: inky red hair and dark eyes and a weird smile that implied he knew shit about me I didn't want him to know. He bummed a cigarette. Few minutes later he nodded at the bathroom. I followed.

Inside a stall I said, "Ask you a favor?"

"Yeah, whatever." Cole took his dick out and began to jerk off.

"Hit me," I said.

"What?"

"Hit me in the face."

Cole stopped jerking off. "Can I still fuck you if I do?"

"Yeah."

Cole balled his hand into a fist. "You ready?"

"Yeah." I steeled myself. A second later my chin felt dislocated and throbbed like a sonofabitch. I tasted blood in my mouth. It was sort of a relief.

"All right?"

"Yeah, hit me again."

"You serious?"

"Do it."

This time Cole socked me below my left eye. I felt a pop and thought for a second my eye had jumped ship, and then I felt my face and my eye was there, but the area underneath had puffed up. Little more relief. "Good, I'm good," I said.

Cole smiled. "So let's fuck."

I turned, then put my hands on the wall above the toilet. Blood dribbled from my mouth to the bowl. Cole jerked my pants down then stuck his finger between my asscheeks to rub my hole.

"Got a condom?" I said. "I'm kind of...in a relationship." I squeezed my eyes shut and shook with the cold sweats.

"Red one, size magnum." Cole chuckled. "Can you handle it?"

"Fine," I said. "Make it hurt."

"You're a weird faggot." Cole opened me up pretty good, and I pressed my nails into the wall until they felt like they'd open like lids.

Cole shoved his cock so far up my ass he pushed my face to the wall. "What a juicy hole," he said. "Maybe you're bleeding." He started to pant, then got incoherent behind me. I wanted him to finish. Just finish. "I'm going to blow," he muttered behind me. *Yeah, do it; I'm a lousy worthless stupid whore.* "Yeah," he said, "yeah."

When Cole finished, I yanked up my pants. He peeled the condom off his dick then flicked it into the toilet. I tried to see come mixing with blood. Cole smacked my ass, startling me.

"Where to, want to crash at the pad?"

"No thanks." What was wrong with me? I hurt all over.

"Well, I don't know why you'd bother going back to the boyfriend. Who'd deal with your shit?"

I grabbed Cole by the throat. "Shut up, shut the fuck up. You don't know anything about him."

Cole threw up his hands. "Fine, let go."

I did.

"Weird-ass faggot," he muttered.

Then I was alone.

I let myself into the apartment. The kitchen was dark. A second later a light came on. I held up a hand. "Damon," he said.

"Hey." After a minute I put my hand down.

"What happened? Did somebody jump you?"

"No, nothing like that."

Asa came over and studied my face. Part of me was so glad to see him I couldn't bear it. He left and came back with a wet rag; I took it. Asa left the room.

Maybe it was the next morning, although I wasn't sure what time it was or what planet I was on initially because my head felt two sizes too big for my body, but Asa woke me. Still dark outside. I managed to say, "What?" Then sort of panicked. Asa stood next to the bed, already dressed. I expected him to hand me a bag of my stuff, as in *this is it*. I think I moaned. I think I shook my head.

"Thought we'd go for a walk," Asa said.

"Where?" My throat hurt.

"Beach, to clear our heads."

I tried to read his tone and couldn't. So I stood out of bed and winced from the pain in my head before I got dressed, jeans and a sweater.

Moments later, we headed down the street. The sky was blue-black like a bruise. For a while Asa kept his hands in his pockets, then he pulled one out and pointed at the sky. "See that constellation there?"

I looked, and the stars blurred like I'd cry or something fucked up like that. I swallowed. "No." Then I stared as hard as I could.

"Looks like a whale," Asa said, directing me to the right.

"Oh right, that big submarine sandwich." I tried to laugh. Asa laughed a little and then said, "C'mon, it's a whale."

"You're right." I sensed him looking at me. We didn't say anything else. Five minutes later we scaled down a cliff to the beach and walked along the water. The sun had begun to rise. I looked at Asa then away when I saw his eyes turn to mine. Ahead about twenty feet near the water I saw something move.

"What's that?"

Asa stopped but didn't answer.

"Is that a seagull?" I looked, trying to see it. "Yeah, it is." The bird hopped cockeyed along the waterline. "It's hurt." I looked over my shoulder at Asa. Our eyes met. A moment later I hurried up the beach toward the bird. It was caught in a net. *How the fuck had that happened?* I dropped to my knees on the sand and the bird hopped in the opposite direction, dragging a piece of net with it. I inched forward to reach for it, and the bird pecked my hand. "Fuck!" I yanked my hand back. "Goddammit!" I shoved my hand out again, and the bird narrowly missed me. "Do it!" I shouted. "Just fucking peck me full of holes!" The bird squawked and then toppled into the water. That was when I lost it: I cried, bent over and choking. Asa was behind me on the sand now. I felt him and wiped my face. The seagull had calmed down enough that Asa was able to flip the net off it. The bird was free.

SHORT SAD SORDID SEXUAL ENCOUNTERS

Sam J. Miller

By the time I finished kneading the dough I
was totally exhausted. Tranced out on the
push and pull of it, I went way past the ten-
minute mark the cookbook mandated. My
muscles were aching and I was out of breath,
and I kept going. Maybe all the extra kneading would make the loaf come out better than
the dense, lumpy, tasteless bread I'd baked in
the past, but that wasn't why I kept going.
Kneading dough spans a whole gamut of emotions: I was massaging my lover's back; I was
punching the president in the face, I was ripping apart the whole status quo. I was a fifties
housewife nourishing her nuclear family. I was
a five-year-old playing with modeling clay.

After the oven heat of the kitchen, our bedroom felt frigid.

"You should try kneading the dough next time," I said. "It's pretty erotic."

No response, not even a tiny fraction of a head nod. When Sprell is working he tunes the world out, which is a trick I can't pull off. I'm very easily distracted. And then again, if Sprell called me or the phone rang while I was in there wrestling the dough, would I have noticed? My upper arms still ached, and my face was glowing.

After a long time Sprell said, "You find *everything* erotic."

The trance was broken. "Let me see," I said.

Our new panel showed a cute blond boy with scruffy hair and a ringer-T, looking exasperated. "But sex is *fun!*" he was saying, splaying out his palms to make the point. In the previous panel, his older, wiser roommate had said, back to the viewer, coffee cup in hand, "I'm just saying maybe you ought to cool it with the random hookups, is all."

"It looks so good," I said. "We have time for two more, and then dinner."

"All right," he said, standing, flexing, joining his hands together high above his head and then leaning back as far as he could—which is not far. Neither of us has seen the inside of a gym since high school phys ed. He sat back down and assumed the monk position, leaning over the frame, his hands moving in slow, small, expert jerks. I had already scripted out the next several panels of our comic book, so I was free to worry about other things.

I went to the window. Grand Concourse was shrouded in fog. In the past two hours a cool damp day had become a frigid November night. I was thirsty, but couldn't brave the kitchen's heat for a glass of water. Through the shoddy metal frame of the window came frigid air, which I desperately needed. Everything about our neat little domestic scene was suddenly supererotic to me: the cluttered table, the poor lighting, the smell of baking bread. It added up to the hardest hard-on I'd ever had—I took deep slow breaths to distract from the urge to unzip.

Intense concentration made it hard to read Sprell's face. Was the work going well? Was he excited or infuriated? He always said faces were the hardest to ink, and watching his while he worked I got his point—I couldn't put that expression into words, let alone draw it. I stared at him; I tried to focus on other things.

We'd written the outline together. Our comic book was full of sex, and it was hard to get much done in a day because the subject matter got us too turned on. Sprell was better at being disciplined. How did he do it? He wasn't much older than me, yet he was master of his libido in ways I could never manage. The night before, he and I had sketched in the hot 'n' heavy sex scene that was the centerpiece of the book.

"Hell of a place," Jerry says, standing in the center of the room in such a way as to show off the seat of his pants.

"Yeah, but it's not mine," Tim says. "I just rent that room over there, from this other guy."

It's four in the morning and Tim is in his normal presex giddy mode. He's trying to remember how to be a good host, but can't keep his mind off Jerry's crotch, Jerry's face, the smell of Jerry's sweat. Blurry flashes of Jerry dancing.

"Is he hot?" Jerry asked. "Does he let you suck him off if you're short on the rent?"

"No, because we don't live in a porno," Tim says, reaching out to cup a hand around the back of Jerry's neck. From his

guest's eyes it's clear he's slightly drunk, and totally smitten.

"What time is he due home?" Jerry asks.

"Are you kidding? He's such an old fart. He's probably been in bed since ten. That's his bedroom over there."

"Well then." Jerry pulls Tim into his arms and they kiss, and Jerry grasps Tim's shoulders. It's clear that Tim wants to prolong the kiss as long as possible, but he does not resist when Jerry starts to push him down onto his knees. Instead he keeps his eyes on Jerry's perfect booze-glazed face until he's at eye level with the Bulge. Jerry unzips, and pulls himself out, but Tim wants to see more. He unbuckles Jerry's belt, pulls pants and boxers all the way down, and begins to unbutton Jerry's tight-fitting overshirt at the same time as he starts sucking. "Dirty boy," Jerry says approvingly, although from then on he does manage to can the porno talk. When he's gotten Jerry totally naked, Tim squeezes his asscheeks like it's a matter of life and death. Even with his mouth so distorted by the size of the thing it's dealing with, you can see from Tim's face how deeply and totally in love he is.

All of which we boiled down to about eight frames. After that we did a long series of close-ups and details that got quite raunchy at times. Many of the frames were meant to leave the reader unsure of what body part was being shown (shoulder? buttock? hip?), but it all gave off a definite sense of throb and intimacy.

Inking tires Strell out almost as much as sex, and he joined me on the couch as soon as the frames were finished.

"How are they?" I asked. I couldn't get up and look for myself on account of his body lying on top of mine.

"Fantabulous," he said sleepily. "How long until the bread is ready?"

"A bit still," I said. "Twenty minutes. You want to take a nap?"

"Is that cool? Just a short one."

"Sure." Earlier in the day he'd made a huge pot of black beans and rice, which had been simmering on the stove for hours and could simmer for hours more. Clumsily, we shifted positions so I could get up without disturbing him once he was asleep. Which happened almost at once. Which is another skill I'm superjealous of.

Our book was about the rocky friendship between gay go-go boy Tim and his older, lonelier, HIV-positive roommate. Tim fell in love with a different boy every night but was weak on the follow-through. The roommate was getting over his lover's death, but because of poverty had to share his mourning with a stranger who could cover the half of the rent his partner had been paying. I was proud of how little these two men resembled Sprell and me, how creative we were to come up with these two interesting fictional characters out of nowhere. But Tim's pain was too familiar: the lust so hard and sharp you can't separate it from love. That much came from me, I was sure, and it was strange to see it on the page and confront it from another angle. And Roommate—never named, never going out, hiding from the world, glimpsed only in fragments— had a grief entirely foreign to me, a depth of feeling I lacked. I didn't know where it came from, and I feared it came from somewhere in Sprell.

Sleeping, Sprell's face went as blank as stone. It was strong, stubbly, masculine. Watching him sleep, I thought of tough young men with nowhere else to go, sleeping on the subway. Another uncanny Sprell ability: to go blank, to hide himself away. When we fought it drove me crazy the way all trace of him vanished, leaving me standing shaking my fist at my own inability to get inside his head. His shaved skull and broad nose, and the wild chest hair that poked up through the collar of his T-shirt, made me feel hopelessly shallow and totally unable to get through to the Real Sprell.

The book felt like having a new baby would feel, for couples who could have one. I imagine. We'd tried to think up a way to make a book about a happy committed gay couple, but there was no drama in that, and neither of us had ever seen a work of art like that. Even in gay films, the taint of porn and misery is everywhere. "Without lots of random hookups and bleak, forlorn, doomed sex scenes," Sprell had said, "we might as well be doing cave paintings. Shit no one will ever see."

I read through what we had so far: fifteen pages, each one the product of a full Saturday or Sunday. In the past couple months we'd hardly gone out at all. Our evenings and our weekends were consumed with the book and with sex, and I had never been happier, and I panicked at the thought of how we would spend our time when it was done.

Pushing PLAY on the VCR conjured up an empty gym. After a rousing round of racquetball, two boys share a glass of milk. The slighter, black-haired boy can't keep his eyes off the bigger blonder one's crotch, which presently swells with a hell of a hard-on. Although they were both gorgeous, I stopped the scene halfway through: I knew how it ended and it wasn't so hot. Not my thing. Sad how well-worn my pornos were, how well I knew each scene and shrug and smile and shudder. I switched tapes.

Three beautiful Brazilian boys. They're in the woods, in a clearing, on a sheet on the ground. One is standing on one leg, caught between a huge Something in his ass and a more reasonably sized Something in his mouth. I'm drawn to the one in the middle, and not just because I find his face cutest. He's the only one whose face shows something other than the two standard emotions of gay porn: fake ecstasy (the guy he's sucking) and fake nastiness (the guy fucking him, barking, in Portuguese, *That's right, suck that cock, yeah, take it, take it you fucking faggot slut*). In little glimpses you can see something like fear at the edges of Middle Man's eyes, and the crazy desperate love I know by heart, the drive to do degrading things, the need to inspire something—pleasure, lust, love, gratitude, contempt—in the blank face of a beautiful man. It's the same look I get even now, after a monogamous year with Sprell, as close to married as they'll let me get for the moment, when I see some stranger sitting across the aisle from me on the subway whose lips and eyebrows and haircut and a million other tiny things make me so weak in the knees that if he stood up and whipped out his cock my mouth would be on it in a flash. The scene fades out and then fades back in, and Middle Man is on his knees between his two lovers, who are standing, instants from orgasm. Sweat shines in the hair of his body, but it's nothing like the other two, who have been sweating so much they look like they've just come out of the ocean churning dully in the background. When they're through, and his face is thoroughly coated with jizz, he smiles a huge, broad, loving smile. I tell myself what all gullible lovers tell themselves: *a smile like that can't be faked*. Then he comes. It's a puny show next to those two juggernauts.

Once I got there myself, and got cleaned up, I headed back into the living room. I petted Sprell's face and his eyes came open. "Hello," I said, sinking into him.

"Hi," he whispered. I cupped him in my arms like a heavy,

fragile, expensive thing I had to carry to safety.

"Where does this come from?" I asked, picking a lump of lint from his navel.

"That's one of the great mysteries of modern life."

I kissed his belly button and then nestled my head on his gut, the way you'd put your ear to a door to eavesdrop. Across the thin membrane I could hear his stomach gurgling, like water in a drain. The thought of what went on in there reminded me how little I understood this thing I held in my hands.

SNOWED IN WITH SAM

Jeff Mann

Every dream must have a setting. This one's snow.

Late January 2005, dusk in the mountains of Southwest Virginia. I park my pickup and stride through deepening white toward the house, a ramshackle old place isolated among oaks. Against the stairs, I stomp my boots to dislodge snow from the treads, and I know Sam must hear the pounding. Because this is my world, the world I've made, what he feels is not dread but delight in knowing I'm home.

Inside, I shoulder off my leather jacket, toss my backpack in the front hall, and head for the kitchen to pour us both a drink. Sam's where I left him, where I've dreamed him to be. He looks up at me. He grins around the rubber ball strapped in his mouth. I take off his cowboy hat—Resistol, black straw, bad-boy signifier—kiss his bald spot, tousle his thinning brown hair, replace the hat, and pour out a tumbler of Bushmills Irish whiskey. The chair creaks as I sit in it heavily, as I lean back and take that first welcome sip.

His name isn't really Sam, but, for the sake of avoiding lawsuits, let's call him that. Not that, outside of my head, he would ever read this story, this book. The guy's married to a beautiful, talented woman, they have several beautiful children. In my heart I'm a criminal, God knows, but my sociopathy isn't translated into action, simply because the legal repercussions would be too great. (And who knows? Like Dostoyevsky's Raskolnikov, I might not be able to bear up under the weight of guilt.) And so, outside of this tale, Sam would never find himself here, bucked and gagged on my kitchen floor. But today that's not his choice, that's mine. I create what I can. In fantasy, at least, at last, the laws of probability have no power.

Today he's here, and he's happy to be here, happy to be my hopelessly helpless boy. Along with the signature cowboy hat, he's got on faded jeans and black cowboy boots. And a slave collar: a short length of chain padlocked around his neck. He's shirtless, needless to say. For me, his hairy chest possesses the power of a religious icon, so of course in my world he's perpetually bare-chested. And tied. A man as beautiful as he is, according to my peculiar leather aesthetic, should be bound almost constantly, and very frequently gagged. Don't ask me why I feel this way. It's as much of a mystery as the constellations' silent revolutions, the sticky bud scales splitting in the spring. Some of you, I know, understand. To use the vernacular I share with my mountaineer brethren, I cain't hep it.

Bucked and gagged? For the vanilla boys out there, it used to be a Civil War torture/punishment. Sam's sitting on the floor. His hands are tied together in front of him. His booted feet are tied together. He's folded up in a hot and hairy package—early Valentine's Day gift to myself—his arms wrapped around his legs and held in place by a wooden dowel roped between the crooks of his elbows and the crooks of his knees. If this weren't fiction, I never would have left Sam tied that way all day, while I taught, sent out poems to magazines, called my partner, attended a committee meeting, and gathered material for my second-year tenure review. Much too uncomfortable a position to endure for long. Once my buddy Everett tied me this way, and I made it to three hours. I was whimpering by then, I who pride myself on how much pain I can take. He kindly ass-fucked me before he untied me.

Outside, the snow is gray with nightfall, a hue I've seen on surf-smoothed shells at Daytona Beach, where my partner John and I occasionally visit his parents. Somewhere, out in all that cold, a mourning dove musters its sad *coo-coo-coo*, sound made over the grave of some Celtic warrior—Diarmuid, maybe, or Tristan—who's died for love. The whiskey feels like rolling oak embers around my tongue. I look down at Sam looking up at me in the last of the light and know that if anything will redeem my petty rages and flaws, it's how deeply I love beauty.

We sit together in the dark's deepening for a while. It's very quiet, the sort of blessed silence snow brings, erasing the world I do not want, which is to say everything outside this room. Sam sighs, as content as I. He rocks a little in his bonds, bites down on the ball in his mouth, and looks up at me, eyes as dark as mine—and isn't this what I've always wanted, to adore a man this beautiful and talented, to control and protect him and see in his eyes that adoration returned? He settles his chin on his chest, the brim of his hat cocked over his eyes. I take another swallow of whiskey, then reach down to stroke his goatee.

His chin's wet with drool. After only a short time, a man with a ball-gag in his mouth starts to drool. Any of you who have read other erotica I've written know what a fetish this is for me. (I cain't hep it.) It certainly is arousing now, with the man I find most desirable on the planet stripped to the waist and roped up at my feet. I rub his goatee, get my fingers good and wet, scrawl my initials on his cheek with his spit. When I bend to kiss him, I bump my forehead on the brim of his hat, so off it comes—placed carefully on the kitchen table at my elbow—and now my beard's brushing his lips, his moist-furred chin, my tongue's running over the ball, over his mustache. Nothing much hotter than kissing a gagged man, especially Sam, feeling him press his mouth against mine, listening to him groan with frustration as he tries without success to work his tongue around the ball—it's buckled in too tight—as he tries to push the gag out. What he wants is his mouth filled not with rubber but my tongue's meat. Soon enough. I lick the tip of his nose, then straighten up and take another sip of whiskey. Smiling, I sit back and nod, and Sam takes his cue. He bares his teeth around the ball and chews on it. He growls and shakes his head from side to side, works up another mouthful of slave-slobber that brims over the corners of his mouth and drips onto his belly. He tugs hard at the ropes holding him in place and growls some more.

Sweet boy: he knows I like to see him struggle. He obliges me, grunting and writhing at my feet. He takes a short break, panting around the ball, breathing heavily through his nose, then starts fighting again, the muscles in his bare shoulders and arms straining with the effort. I watch in silence, and the windows fill with lavender twilight.

After a good ten minutes, Sam's armpits are musky-moist—damn, he smells good, like spices and forest loam. His chin, chest, belly, and crotch are wet with sweat and drool, and both his cock and mine are thick in our jeans. Exhausted, he surrenders, hangs limply in his bonds. I reach over, place my hand over his hairy chest, and feel the racing of his heart.

Time for his reward. I pat him on the head, kiss him on his sweat-streaked brow, and then gently unbuckle the gag and pull it out.

"Thanks!" Sam whispers. I wait while he works the stiffness out of his jaw. Tipping the tumbler of Bushmills to his lips, I let him take a sip. Sam slurps greedily at the liquid gold, and a little spills over, joining the saliva in his chest hair. I wipe up the whiskey with a forefinger, run my finger around a nipple, then push my finger into Sam's mouth. He sucks on it for a second, then I pull his head back by his hair and press my mouth to his.

Sam groans and opens his mouth to me. This time our kiss is untrammeled. Tongue to tongue, beard to beard. It goes on for a while, the kind of passion I thought I could no longer feel or find. Pretty soon my face is smeared with his saliva, and we're both grinning and nibbling mustaches and lips. Every now and then I take a sip more Bushmills, give him another nip, and then we're off again, filling one another, probing mouths scented with whiskey. What bliss he brings me. In this word-world, what bliss I bring him.

We're both a little buzzed. The snow has thickened considerably during our tongue-fest, lining the limbs of the maple outside the kitchen window. Time to get dinner on, or we'll never eat. I swig the last of the whiskey, hold it in my mouth, then kiss Sam a final time, pushing the liquor between his lips. He sips the burning from my tongue, swallows hard, and closes his eyes.

I reach for the gag on the kitchen table and am about to buckle it back in when he opens his eyes and says, "Wait. Wait, please."

"Yep?" I kiss his shoulder, the gag hanging from my hand.

"Why am I here?" He opens his eyes and looks up at me, yearning, confused, as if he's just forgotten something momentous.

"Because I'm imagining this." Between his goatee and his sideburns, a few days' worth of beard-stubble darkens his cheeks, and I brush it softly with the back of my hand.

Sam licks his lips. He kisses my hand, then turns his head and stares out into the snow. "Go on," he says quietly.

"Because this is the only way I can have you. Because, if I had the power of a god, this is what I would most want, out of all the world's erotic permutations and possibilities. Because you're my Muse."

Sam nods. "I understand." He gazes out into the snow a moment longer, then looks at me solemnly and says, "Please, would you gag me again?"

Tenderly I push the ball against his lips. He smiles—wistful, I think is the word for that expression—and opens his mouth, takes the black ball between his teeth. As I buckle it behind his head, Sam mumbles "Thank you." I sit there beside him in the dark for a while. Sam leans his head against my knee, and we listen to the wind come up, splintering the snow-silence that's prevailed until now, thundering the tin roof, lashing the windowpanes with snow.

We're both Southern boys, country boys—Louisiana, Virginia—that's part of the attraction. So I know without asking—delicious how he's in no position to speak, delicious the muffled replies he'd manage if I did ask—what kind of meal he'd relish on a cold night like tonight. I like to cook for my roped-up boy. First, some music: I slide *A Celtic Tale* into the CD player. Then a little more whiskey. What a combination of the perverse and the domestic: a drink in hand, a handsome, goateed slave, snow making parlous the roads, and a big down-home meal of barbequed ribs, cole slaw, kale, and cornbread. Hell, I'm the architect of my own paradise.

You're missing a fine time if you haven't been in Sam's boots, if you haven't been tied up and cooked for by a man like me. The sauce I simmered yesterday, the greens I cleaned this morning, and pretty soon the ribs are in the oven, the slaw's shredded, and the kale is simmering with fatback. I sit at the kitchen table by a reading lamp and read a little of *Seven Viking Romances*. Every now and then I pull the gag out long enough to give Sam another sip of whiskey. Every now and then I run my fingers through the hair on his chest, flicking and tugging his nipples till they harden and the front of his jeans swells, till he closes his eyes, throws back his head, nods with pleasure, and groans gratitude into his gag. The furnace cuts on with increasing regularity—I have the heat up so Sam will be comfortable shirtless—which tells me the temperature's continuing to drop. Tonight, Sam and I will have one another, flannel sheets, and my great-aunt's homemade quilts to keep us warm.

We're both really drunk now, and my intoxication is quadrupled by his bare torso, his handsome face, the smell of his armpits, his quiet submission. This fiction is what I've been waiting for, an excuse to have Sam, not a substitute, not a surrogate. And this is the miracle this little story allows: he's both willing and eager. He's not some distant, famous Nashville star who doesn't know I exist. This, I think, rolling one nipple between thumb and forefinger till Sam groans, must be the sweet comfort the full-fledged psychopath enjoys. What good is the present state of virtual-reality technology if it can't give me this, a weekend snowed in with Sam?

Every fantasy is a monologue, and since Sam and I are both happy with him gagged, it's a monologue he gets now, as I sit here, lights off again, a few candles lit, wind hammering the house and tossing the line of pines against the horizon back of the house. Sam leans his head against my thigh, I stroke his chest and his brow, I talk and he listens.

I tell him about attending his Charleston concert last fall, standing in that packed civic center with thousands of sex-crazed women, young and old, whose screaming shenanigans made my passion for him seem moderate in contrast. I saw him pull off his sweat-drenched shirt after the last song, when he was halfway down the corridor leading backstage. I watched his smooth, broad, bare shoulders receding into the distance and disappear around the corner and I wanted so badly to follow him, to make love to him in whatever Kanawha Valley hotel he was staying in that night.

I tell him about "The Quality of Mercy," the novella I wrote last spring, in which my protagonist, an obsessed ex-convict named Sean, fictionalized version of Jeff, kidnaps West Virginia country singer Tim, fictionalized version of Sam.

I tell him about the little Sam-shrine I have in my office: the baseball cap with his name stitched into it, the little ceramic tile with that hot picture that graced the cover of his last CD.

Sam in black cowboy hat, black coat, black shirt open to his solar plexus, revealing the meaty curve of his left pec matted with dark hair, a maddening glimpse of nipple if you look closely enough.

I point out the photos of him stuck to my refrigerator, tell him about the Sam calendar on the wall by my bed, where he and I will be sleeping together later. In my closet, there are T-shirts with his name on them, "Sam-wear" I bought at the online fan store. There's a black cowboy hat a lot like his that I wear with my drover when the weather warms up. Sometimes I see it on the table in the front hall and can pretend that Sam just took it off, that he's around the house somewhere, that we live together, that he's my lover. There's a Sam sticker on the rear window of my pickup truck. And, of course, I own all his CDs and even play some of his songs on the piano and guitar.

I get a little worked up, explaining my ardor. "Nothing better than driving mountain roads in my pickup, listening to your CDs! The way you say *cain't* and *thang*, just like me, makes me feel at home. Some of those songs, hell, I get so excited I start letting loose with Rebel Yell yee-haws of delight! Your voice, it's like you're there, you know? Like we're travel buddies. I listen to your music and look at your photos, and think, Shit, this is crazy, his voice is right here with me, so why cain't his body be? Why cain't I touch his body the way his voice touches me?! Y'know?!"

Sam sits through this mumbled worship, grinning moistly around his gag, occasionally rolling his eyes but clearly impressed with, flattered by, my fanaticism. I can tell by the serenity in his gaze that he realizes that I'm no threat. He's no more in danger than a god in the presence of his priest.

What this confession, these relics, indicate is not insanity but passion. I'm in love. I'm just like all those hysterical women in the Charleston Civic Center last October, dreaming of a passionate, deeper, more fulfilling life, craving what they can never have, longing for what they find most beautiful. It's the common lot of humanity. Some of us are just more honest than others about what we want. Some of us are just more enamored of the inaccessible and the perverse.

The timer goes off; the ribs are done. I pull them out to cool, mix up cornbread batter and pour it into a heated cast-iron skillet, and in half an hour we're ready to eat. More music, the soundtrack to *Rob Roy*. Don't want to embarrass Sam by playing his CDs all evening, and besides, we both have Irish blood, so I figure we're predisposed to like Celtic music. The wind's still rattling the roof, and now there's the weary scrape of a snowplow on the road down the hill. I like the sound. It emphasizes the cozy isolation Sam and I share.

Great advantage to being a bondage top in fiction: no awkward fumbling with knots, no tying and untying. Simple shift of a paragraph, and now Sam's bound in an entirely different manner. (What is good kink but working some variety into the demandingly tight constrictions of fetish?) He's sitting beside me on a kitchen chair, within arm's reach so I can feed him easier. He's barefoot now, still shirtless, in a pair of black jeans with ragged rips in the knees and thighs, revealing the brown hair on his legs. His wrists are crossed behind his back and knotted together. There's a good bit of cotton rope wrapped around his torso, securing his arms to his sides, cinching his elbows together. The white cords make his chest-pelt look even thicker and darker, his pecs even meatier. The gag's different too: his mouth's bisected by a thick bit—nothing much prettier than the juxtaposition of that goatee, the tender bow of those full lips, and that rubber rod between his teeth.

Around the kitchen I light more candles. I reach over, gently tug the slave chain around his neck. "Time to eat," I say, unbuckling the bit.

I feed Sam with my fingers, just as my protagonist did the man he kidnapped, in the novella my yearnings for Sam inspired. Good to be doing it myself, rather than through a fictional persona. He's as hungry as I am, eagerly taking from my fingers the rich bits of barbequed country-style ribs and buttered cornbread. I lift spoonfuls of kale to his lips, he slurps the pot liquor. We're drinking Bud Light, his favorite beer, and, as much of a beer snob as I am, I have to admit that the clean taste works well with spicy barbeque sauce.

"Damn, this is good," he sighs. "Kinda food I grew up on. Fighting your ropes really worked up my appetite. Gimme another swig of that beer."

It's a messy meal, and soon I've got a barbeque stain on my white T-shirt. At Sam's request, I shuck it off. Now we're both bare-chested in this warm space, grinning drunkenly, happy to be together, while the blizzard rattles the windowpanes and the silhouettes of trees waver in and out of white. When Sam gets sauce on his furry chin, I laugh and lick it off. When my mustache gets buttery, he leans forward grinning— "C'mere"—and licks me clean.

"Pretty awkward," Sam says at one point, as he angles his head to tug meat off a bone I proffer him.

"You want me to untie you?"

"Hell, no!" He flexes his chest and arms in their web of rope. "This feels great. Keep me this way as long as you want."

"You really are my creature," I say, tugging the meat off for him and slipping it in his open mouth. Pygmalion must have felt like this.

"Guess so!" Sam laughs. "Jeff, dribble a little of that honey on my cornbread, okay? And how 'bout a shot of hot sauce on those greens?"

We're too busy eating to talk much, and by the time we're done, it's late. There's a pile of cleaned bones on our plates, half the cornbread is gone, we're belching softly, and I've unbuckled both his belt and mine. The snow shows no sign of slowing.

I lift Sam to his feet, wipe his mouth with a paper towel, and wrap my arms around him. His bare chest against mine is warm, moist, and soft with hair. We're just about the same height, and I rest my chin on his shoulder, clasp his roped wrists between my fingers. "So, if such an idyll were real, if you and I together could ever come to be, what do you think we'd talk about?"

He grins. "Hell, you're the author. You tell me!"

"Country living, country music?"

"Yeah."

"Fathers. How they hurt."

"Yeah..."

"Pickup trucks, motorcycles..."

"Yeah!"

"What would we do together? Maybe drink some beer, eat some chips and dip, watch some football?"

"Sounding good!"

"I could play the guitar while you sang?"

"Yep, whatever you want. That'd be fun."

"I Immmm, guess I don't know you well enough to put convincing words in your mouth," I say, unzipping his jeans and tugging them to his ankles. "Think I'll skip the dialogue and fill my mouth instead."

His nipples are soft and hard at once, anointed with left-over sauce. Tonight, in this snowstorm, in this sentence, at last I lick them, softly at first, then, at his urging, harder. He's made to like it rough. I take his pecs in my hands and massage their meatiness hard, just this side of being brutal. I suck his areolas, bite the very tips of his nipples till he's groaning, wincing, hissing with pain and with rapture. I range a little, my beard-fur mingling with the wet hairiness between his tits, with the crest of fur along his belly, then I'm back to his nipples, brushing them with my cheek-stubble, lapping and teeth-tugging them raw, like some hungry god taking his turn at a bowl of ambrosia.

When Sam starts to make little sobbing sounds, I finally desist. I take a long pull of beer, give the same to him, and drop to my knees for the next course. I've been wanting to suck his cock for years now. Last fall, standing in that crowded civic center as Sam sang, I watched him lift his shirt every now and then to give us teasing flashes of bare belly, and I knew that his chest, his cock, his ass were the ones, of all men's on earth, that I most wanted to devour.

I tease us both by chewing and licking the swell in his boxer briefs for a minute or two before peeling them down and letting the heft of his cock pop free. His dick's long and thick, the kind that lean, rangy men like him tend to have. I drip honey on the rosy tip, delicately lap it off, then slide the whole length in—sword sliding into the scabbard meant for it—till I choke. I back off a bit, chew on the head a little, then start a regular rhythm along the shaft, with occasional tongue-swirls over the head and into the piss-slit. A man like me's well-practiced, and in no time at all Sam's getting close, fucking the back of my throat hard and fast. He's making a lot of moaning music, good excuse for me to grab bondage tape and a bandana off the sideboard.

"About time," he growls. He puts up a few sweet seconds of mock-resistance, just the way I like it, before I force the bandana between his teeth and knot it tightly behind his head. One, two, three, four layers of tape over his mouth, around his head, the end cut off with a kitchen knife. "Mmmm mmm," he says, nodding, blinking at me as I smooth the shiny blackness over his lips.

The dishes go flying beneath my forearm. They hit the floor and shatter. Licked and gnawed rib-bones scatter over linoleum. But—the convenience of fiction again—no one needs to clean up. The fragments disappear with the sound of their shattering.

Table's cleared now. I spin Sam around, bend him over the table, and spread his ass cheeks. They're softly hairy, and the cleft is a puff of black smoke. I knead his buttocks, brush one fingertip between them. When I reach his hole, he tenses beneath my touch. I drop to my knees, bite one cheek, then the other. He grunts, clenches and unclenches his bound hands. The height of fantasy, a universe in which we both want me inside him.

His ass tastes as good as it smells—black walnuts, buckwheat honey, orchard grass, granite. I tease his hole only briefly, then push my tongue in as far as it will go. Beneath the muffling layers of tape, he's shouting. He pushes his ass back against me, his hole spreads open a bit more, my tongue moves further inside.

"Oh God, oh God, oh God." I think that's what he's saying. It's hard to tell.

"Time for bed, Sam," I say, abruptly rising to my feet. Obedient, the candles snuff out one by one. Crooking one finger under the chain of his slave collar, I grip his arm and pull him off the table and to his feet, then help him step out of the ankle-manacles of his peeled-down jeans and briefs.

He stands quietly before me, entirely naked now. Lean, muscular, furry—I can't imagine a man being more desirable. Sometimes God does such fine work. Damnation, how long have I wanted him like this? Stripped, roped and taped, waiting for me to touch him again. I take his nipples between my fingers—gently now, because I know they're raw. Our eyes meet. What other reward could the afterlife offer? How can there be a paradise without the flesh, its ardors and appetites? Sam hangs his head and presses it to mine. For a long time I simply stand there, soothing his nipples and kissing the top of his head.

In reality, despite my regular weight-lifting, I doubt that this next move would be possible, certainly not for very long—plus, at age forty-five, I have to watch my back, and lately a tendon in my left forearm is screwed, despite the glucosamine I pop like candy. But none of those quotidian concerns matters here. Loving Sam makes me feel manly and strong, young, dominant, protective. Wrapping one arm around his back, another under his knees, I lift him into my arms.

"I'll take care of you," I whisper into his ear. Sam nods. "Mmmm mmm," he murmurs. I can feel the tension leaving his muscles. His head nestles in the space between my shoulder and my jaw.

I stand there in the dark for a full minute, feeling his breath against my neck. There's a pattering against the window-glass. Sounds like the snow is shifting to ice. With any luck we'll be snuggled in here together for days.

I carry Sam into the bedroom and lower him gently into flannel sheets. Blinds pulled down on the soft tick of ice, candles lit around the room. Sam's eyes look moist in the candlelight, glistening like volcanic glass.

Off come my lumberjack boots, my jeans and briefs, and now I'm stretched out in bed beside him. Sam shivers—suddenly the room's chilly—so I pull the sheets over us. We lie there together, listening to the ice, to the snowplow's distant scrape returning. "You all right?" I ask, kissing the tape over his mouth, once, then twice. Sam rubs his face against my chin, against my lips. He nods. He's still shivering, though, so I pull him close, our bodies stretched out together, chest to chest, belly to belly. He closes his eyes, then I close mine.

We've been dozing, I realize. The ice is still clicking, only yards away in the darkness. I reach for Sam, and he's there, back to me now, rubbing his ass against my cock, his roped hands tugging on my belly hair. I wrap one arm around his chest, cup a pec, squeeze. With my other hand, I work his hard cock for a while, till he's groaning and squirming in my embrace.

One fingertip up his ass. "Yeah? You want this, right?" Sam nods and keeps nodding, pushes back until my finger slides entirely in. A second, then, very carefully, a third. He's still wet from the efforts of my tongue, so only a little spit's needed. I work his hole gently—he's very tight, and I know beyond a shadow of a doubt that he's never been fucked before, he's been saving himself for a man who loves him as much as I do.

"Slow, slow, please Sir, slow?" I'm sure that's what those tape-trammeled noises mean.

He's ready now. "Slow, you bet, sweet boy," I whisper. I

grip his furry pec hard. It's wet with sweat, forest moss after a rain. The smell of him washes over me—his pits, his crotch, the musk of his slowly opening ass. Freeze us here, in eternity, like the lovers on the Grecian urn, like the golden birds of Byzantium.

I pinch his nipple hard. Sam grunts. I slide my bunched fingers out of his ass, then push them in again. I slide them out a final time, bite his earlobe, whisper, "You ready to be fucked?"

More nods. "Yes, Sir. Yes, Sir. Please, Sir."

My cockhead, all of its existence up till now far from him, beyond him, outside him, exiled. Pressed now against his hole. And now...and now...just the head inside him. Inside his tightness, his volcanic flesh. Home.

Very slowly I slide farther inside. Sam's groan is continuous now. "All right?" I ask, shifting one hand to his hard-on, clamping the other over his tightly taped mouth. "Yes, Sir." I can hear him inside my head, hear him begging for all of it. Sam rotates his hips, bucks back, and his ass swallows my cock whole.

He's whimpering a little, hurting a little. "Easy, Sam, easy. Relax," I soothe, licking the back of his neck. I hold him hard in my arms, keeping very still till he grows accustomed to being filled with me. We've waited all our lives for this, one man's body inside the body of the other. This is the rightness of rain reaching the dark thirst of root hairs deep in the earth, the inevitability of sunflower fields shifting hour after hour toward the sun.

When Sam nods, I begin a slow fucking, pushing as deeply into him as our bodies' laws will allow. I work his cock, I torture his tits, I grip his taped mouth and pull his head against my lips. I lick the sweat on his scalp, bite his neck and shoulders till they bruise—I want him marked tomorrow. I roll him onto his belly, spread his thighs, and mount him that way, my heavy ardor stretched out along his naked length. Then Sam's on his back with his legs over my shoulders, our eyes interlocked as I shove inside him again and again, bending down to nip at his chest and lap the tape across his face. Then, finally, back onto our sides, jerking his cock with my spit-wet fist, his tightness maddening me. Before I know it, I've lost all control, I'm growling, he's roaring, I'm pounding his ass as hard and as fast as I can.

Far too soon, my hand's dripping with his semen and my semen's filled his ass. We lie there, sides heaving, sweat-slippery, catching our breath. For a long time I stay inside him, letting my cock slowly soften. Meanwhile, I lift my hand to my mouth and lick off every pearl. The furnace hums on again. I pull the sex-rumbled blankets over us, pull Sam against me.

"You comfortable like this?"

"Mmmm mmm."

Of course he is. Fiction—hands tied tight behind him, but no numbness, no aching shoulders. He'll be fine roped and taped all night.

"Lots of ice out there. You're gonna have to stay awhile. How about buckwheat cakes, maple syrup, and bacon for breakfast?"

"Mmmm!" Sam snuggles even closer. For the time we have left, we want no space between us.

I hold Sam till his breathing slows with sleep. Again I cup his hairy breast in my palm and feel his heart beat. I kiss his hair and whisper many things to him in the fitful candlelight. How much I wish him and his family well outside this room, how much pleasure it's given me to listen to his music, admire images of him, love him from afar. How welcome the longing that star-worship allows such ciphers as I, what a surprise it's been to find another Muse this late in life, albeit far-distant and likely never to be met. He sleeps peacefully on, while outside the snowplow scrapes by again, and the silence left in its wake says that the ice has stopped, our isolated idyll is ending, and the roads will be open soon.

Snowbound silence is more eloquent than most speech. Tonight it tells me that I am aging, that some lovers are lost before they are ever found, that some things—the things wanted most—are irremediably unreal, never to be possessed. The silence tells me that no one can escape the mundane, that tomorrow I will wake sober and alone, back to an existence where the greatest beauties remain intolerably far from me.

I slip from bed, careful not to wake Sam. I snuff the candles, then stand by the window and stare out over the fallen snow. The blue shadows thrown by the limbs of oaks are splayed fingers, arms thrown wide for an embrace. I sit on the bed-edge and savor Sam's sleep, his dark eyebrows, his beard-stubbly face, the sound of his slow breath. The same world that almost always denies us what we most desire gives us this consolation, to imagine down to the tiniest detail what raptures our realities will never allow. Gently I touch his goateed chin and the black tape over his mouth. What I tell the silence is that these words are bonds, knots. To hold us together—two men who will never meet, whose passions are irreconcilable—to hold us here. What I tell the silence is that I will make my own miracles, make the moments that Fate will not.

The winter night does not reply. And so I sit here, studying my beloved in his sleep. Outside the snow stretches on, without mark or flaw this late at night, blank as what is left of a page after the story ends, after the mediation of syllables stops and there are no words left to stand between the writer and the world.

RUSHING TIDE OF SANITY

Charlie Vazquez

Manhattan: Winter, 2007
I lip-locked with a British punk stud in an East
Village dive while Kirsty MacColl warned of
chasing bad boys over the shitty speakers—she
and I, apparently, both helpless in our ways.
Shane's sweat was a magnetic force that drew
my lips to his neck, mouth and the bristle
around his ears. His heaving core (like an alien
about to burst out of his chest) and my long
lapses between inhalations of dank air fused
together like a courtship ritual dance of manic
flightless birds. We left and resumed our noisy
pas de deux in the cab's backseat.

At his hotel, I initiated the first of many
prickly kisses to follow; he hadn't shaved in
a couple of days. He let me lead the dance,
which I was used to doing anyway. I opened

the two buttons holding his shirt up and it fell to the floor like a lopsided theater curtain; a crimson screen of animated tattoos came to life on the stage of his torso when the flickering red lights of the hotel across the street splashed their net of light across us. He kicked his shirt out of the way with his dirty boot and surprised me when he pulled me to him by my wrists, chest to chest.

Our mouths wrestled for dominion, neither of us willing to back down. I rested my hands on the top of his head when I gave in—melting had never felt better. That's how I remember surrendering—I melted into him. It's what I needed and I knew it—I was usually the boss. But not this time. No way. The sweaty bristle on his head was all the aphrodisiac I needed. This was the kind of man I idealized: a cocksucking warrior, a man-fucking descendant of Northern European barbarians who had his image burned into my crosshairs.

Shane shoved me against the wall and tore off my grimy T-shirt, the loud ripping signaling a bone-deep sense of awe and danger. He threw the useless cloth behind him, pulled me away from the wall, and pushed me backward onto the couch. Metal jangled. Magician's hands. He handcuffed my wrists over my head, the cold metal stinging. It was done before I realized it, and the unexpected switch was an extraordinary delight: every aggressor has a unique style, and I would soon catch a fantastic glimpse of his. Little did I know I would stew in it.

As he bit me—¡*Maldita sea la madre!*—I was instructed to address my "boss" as Master Hawk. His advance was swift. The torture of his rough sucking and the scraping of his teeth on my skin sent me into soul-stirring distress. I writhed in equal parts misery and euphoria. The process of surrender began. Wave after wave of ancient music emanated from our cores and through our mouths: the tones of his slick and deep sucking—the ebbing. My guttural heaving for relief—the flowing. In tandem, we were in complete and complex bliss.

I was forbidden to cum.

He fitted me with a restrictive locked cock-cage. *Master Hawk locked my cock away from my hands and the rest of the world!* I started to beg for release, stopped. He uncuffed me and told me to dress. When I was done he cuffed my wrists behind my back. Master Hawk then stripped off his jeans, revealing even more of the inky mosaics of his tattoos—and his sexual fury, which strained up, a veiny reverential salute. He pulled a black NYPD police uniform from his closet, complete with belt, cap, holstered handgun, and nightstick.

Master Hawk had plans. "Stand," he demanded while tucking in his shirt.

I stood, awkwardly.

"Forward."

I did exactly as he said, not more, not less.

"Again," he said while fastening his belt.

I stepped forward until I was face-to-face with him; I oozed at the sight of him in full dress, suppressed my pantings of desire. He uncuffed me and pressed my hands to his swollen crotch—his zone of unresolved pleasure. He kissed me deeply, then spit a slimy cannonball of snot-tinted saliva through my teeth and into my mouth; it tasted like beer.

"Swallow."

I did.

"About face..." I was again handcuffed, this time blindfolded, and led out the door, down the hallway, into the elevator, through the lobby, and onto the street. We boarded a taxi. The driver, I'm sure, added us to his "freaky work stories" category. Master Hawk barked an address. The driver didn't murmur a word. Neither did the Master. The suspense of barreling down midtown streets and avenues, blindfolded and handcuffed, in the middle of the night, thrilled me.

When we arrived, Master Hawk guided me to a freight elevator and we ascended what seemed like ten floors before stopping with a harrowing jerk. I could smell old wood in the air—even mildew and mold. A second voice greeted him; they kissed, I surmised during a brief pause; they discussed "the others."

I heard the breathing of a fourth person.

I was instructed to stand against a pole. Master Hawk kissed me roughly, then the man who had greeted him kissed me; their beards were like steel brushes against my face. Cold beer splashed over me, then my ankles were shackled to the wooden post, splinters ripping into my skin. The cuffs were loosened, then my hands were reshackled in front of my crotch. My cock swelled against the painful restriction of its cage. A bag filled with bottles clattered onto a table, then I heard the unmistakable sound of someone writhing in pain.

"Let's let them see," Master Hawk said.

Our blindfolds were lifted. Three of us were bound to the pole in a triangle. A mustached, muscular, heavily tattooed man of Mediterranean mold was to my right; he was dark with thick black body hair. The base of his hard cock was encircled by a leather-studded cock ring. He sneered.

To my left was a towering black man, hairless, muscled and soaking wet; he too had been splashed with beer, or he was sweating. He had short bleached hair and jailhouse-tattooed biceps scribbled with reapers, tombstones and gang script. He regarded me blankly.

The three of us would be forced to work as a team, in order to serve our bosses. Secretly (or maybe not), we were better off bound the way we were. We would have caused each other untold harm—in order to more selfishly please our masters. That is how determined we were, it was in our eyes.

After taking in the physiques and demeanors of my slave peers, I turned my gaze to Master Hawk's companion. I was taken aback. The second master was a rural warrior from Appalachia or the deserts of Oregon or even Australia's outback. He wore a light gray shirt with EARL written in cursive red script over his left pec. The shirt's armpits were soaked with sweat and his dark blue slacks were marred with grease, a formidable erection evident against the classic worker's fabric. "Earl" was barrel-chested with slicked-back, salt-and-pepper brown hair, a tail of curls dropping from the nape of his neck, with two days of torturous stubble—little spears of gray piranha teeth—on his fierce face.

We were told to call him Baron Trash.

Master Hawk's eyes met mine when I finished taking in the scenario. He approached, forced me to stand tall, then bound me to ceiling restraints, turned to face the pole. He dragged my blindfold back into place and kissed me roughly, from the back of my neck to the cheeks of my ass, his serpent tongue darting in and out, before biting into my armpits, savoring them deeply. Then he drew back from his consumption of me, and the thick tips of his leather flogger tickled my face.

The whip was like an oscillating weapon. Its featherlike tips were as soft as cilia on first contact, but soon accelerated to a force that battered my upper back and then my ass like a boxer's rolling, pounding fist, faster and stronger, next landing with a hissing crash on my left shoulder. I tried to kneel to my left, but was restrained by my bindings.

Something within me collapsed and I allowed myself to fall with it. The skull-rattling blows transitioned to thinner strands that tore at my skin more greedily—cat's claws dragging through skin, razor tips carving designs into flesh. Master Hawk had replaced his original whip with another, one that lashed at my back in horizontal swipes, biting stings from the left and hungry slices from the right. My skin was at once hot and cold. Each strike was preceded by the snakelike hiss of cutting air, which added to the glorious anticipation. My body convulsed. I was more alive with each strike.

Baron Trash unshackled the darkest slave; I heard him crawl forward, heard him slurp on Master Hawk's cock. My Master moaned. I recognized the sound of his breathing and I hated the slave who was sucking my Master's cock, torn by his pleasure at what should be rightfully *mine!*

The sound of Master Hawk's approaching orgasm filled my ears as the full-lipped slave worked his cock like a machine— every wet slurp sounding as though it were happening inches before me. Master Hawk made him stop and struck him in the ass with the nightstick. I was then able to make out the sound of Baron Trash feeling the reward of pleasure seize his fat and dirty dick, as the kneeling slave went to work on him instead. It was apparent that the bare concrete floors stung the slave's knees; his breathing was tinted with a pain he tried to subdue beneath his duty.

The hairy third slave was unbound and forced to suck Master Hawk—I was, by that time, able to tell what was happening by employing the rest of my senses. My jealousy surfaced at the worst of times. I was not allowed to communicate that—though I knew that Master Hawk felt it thickly in the air and was delighted by it. He then instructed the Greek-looking punk slave to lick his balls and boots and accept delicious verbal humiliations, which the Greek slave seemed to derive great pleasure from; his servicing became more enthusiastic with the worsening of the verbal insults.

I was deprived of worshipping the masters at all—I'd been granted a severe punishment. My need for sex became a burning torture in my crotch: I was done with the mind games and was ready to come, but I would need to learn to wait. My deprivation hatched imaginary outcomes in my mind—as to what the rest of the night would lead to.

Our blindfolds were removed again. The black man's mammoth cock was majestically erect. The hairy man's equally massive erection was fleshy and red around the head. My cock was still at bay, incarcerated. We were made to kneel. Master Hawk and Baron Trash set three metal dog bowls down and filled them to overflowing with beer. I knew better than to move. The hairy man did not. He was whipped by the Baron for sipping without first awaiting directions. His bowl of beer was dumped over his head, filled again, put to his mouth, and again dumped over his head, a cruel reenactment of the Curse of Tantalus.

The other slave and I were allowed to drink our beer as a reward. Then all three of us were manhandled into a cage in the center of the room, an enclosure so confining we could only hunch on all fours, side by side, our muscles bunched, our faces strained.

Master Hawk's posture was telling; his shoulders were spread apart, his crotch was pointed forward and his hands rested on his hips, as if examining a situation requiring intervention. The near future was already in his eyes. Baron

Trash and Master Hawk unzipped their trousers and showered us with zigzags of warm urine tinted with the unmistakable stench of beer. The chattering cascades of piss were accompanied by their sighs of relief and pleasure, coupled with our very own childish squeals of joy. We were men broken into boys.

When they were done, we were dragged from the cage and the splintered post, piss dripping from our bodies. Master Hawk poured beer over my head—and almost as instantly—licked up the foaming nose-diving cascades. Baron Trash did the same to the black slave and I wondered how the Greek-looking slave felt as Master Hawk made sure to slurp up beer from my armpits, chest, ass and legs. The Greek glared at me.

The cold beer made me shiver.

"Do you have to piss, boy?" Master Hawk asked.

I nodded.

"Then piss."

I was scared—I wasn't sure if I'd been given permission or if I was being tricked. But I lost control of my bladder anyway as another wave of cold beer washed over my head. I shivered uncontrollably as Master Hawk sank to his knees to take in my urinary rush. He held some in his mouth, rose slowly to his feet, and forcefully spat it back in my face.

The feisty Baron then went over to his Greek slave and said, "Hello."

The slave returned the greeting—feeling pressured to speak—and then screamed out for forgiveness when the Baron squeezed the cock ring that encircled his genitals—the kind with studs that dig into sensitive skin.

"You weren't given permission to speak," the Baron growled to the hairy slave.

The slave sank to his knees in a sort of comical Hollywood misery—his face contorting with a severe will not to speak. Our blindfolds were taken away and I wondered what Master Hawk and Baron Trash had planned next. My need for pleasure became a testicular pain, a tension with only one remedy.

What came next relieved my tension. We were to have sex with one another, while my Master and the Baron watched.

The Greek was ordered by the Baron to suck the black slave's enormous curved dick, as the masters masturbated, all the while cruelly critiquing their live sex show. When they'd had enough I was told to eat the Greek's ass while the black slave sucked him. Master Hawk momentarily freed me of the cock-cage—*qué milagro!* This carnal musical chairs went on for what seemed like hours. We were forbidden to come— though we raced closely to it at times, mentally drawing back, communicating through natural sounds of the body that we were flirting with disaster.

When the masters had had enough, I was instructed to kneel before the Baron, the black slave before Master Hawk. The Greek lingered behind us, shivering in a puddle of piss, beer and sweat. We were freed of our handcuffs and told to unzip the masters before us and "finish them off." I happened to look over at the black slave as he put Master Hawk's dick in his greedy mouth. Baron Trash caught a whiff of my jealousy and slapped my cheek to remind me of what I was supposed to be doing.

During the grueling session before my second master, I talked myself out of believing what I thought I was hearing. The masters seemed to be coordinating their arousal. The sound of their approaching orgasms became louder as we synchronized to form a team. We were as two turbines sifting the same current.

Master Hawk then commanded the Greek to put a rubber on and fuck the black slave; I still wasn't sure why I was being left out of so much. The Greek was allowed to come, and he came in a consistent and building bombardment of the black slave's ass—in endless and greedy grunts of relief, he slipped off his target and leapt back onto it, like a crazed dog. The dark slave barely squinted as this happened and continued suckling. The Baron poured more beer on my head, set his bottle down and groaned from a deep place. Master Hawk heaved deeply, spoken language eluding his tongue.

The masters then rushed simultaneously; each leading the other upward in pulsating fits of ancient ecstasy, their loud moaning mounting in length and volume. The Baron anchored his greasy hands onto the back of my head—to make sure my mouth wouldn't separate from his boiling pleasure. The masters came in a duo of operatic beauty—two commanding basses bending to sensitive tenor. They barely relinquished control and gave out orders as soon as their eruptions of passion had passed and dripped from our eager lips.

The Greek had come as well as our masters. The black slave and I hadn't and I was deeply wounded when Master Hawk had me crawl over to him so he could put my cock-cage back on. He tongued me passionately, in wide arcs of dominion. The black slave was told to masturbate. The slicked, gliding motion of his fingers and hand around his remarkable member entranced me.

He locked eyes with me. We communicated visually. Our souls had sex through the intercourse of our uninterrupted stare: I at times staring deeper, he at times surpassing my intensity. I perceived what I believed to be an effort on his part to soften his stance—in order for him to orgasm. I could feel him retreating from—what seemed like—an occupation of my conscience. I then played my silent role as alpha slave: I had the final word, as far as slaves were concerned, and my sneer, stare and stiffness would show it.

The dark slave then shuddered madly; he fell to his side as explosions seized hold of him—he came repeatedly into a puddle of piss and beer while staring through my eyes at a dimension behind me. Master Hawk and Baron Trash seemed impressed. The three of us were uncuffed and handed our clothes and knapsacks. Master Hawk demanded I wait for him once I was done. It wasn't yet clear if our roles had been terminated for the night or if we were still under their command.

I showered—barely.

The other slaves left without cleaning up at all.

I never found out what happened to Baron Trash.

Shane and I taxied back to the hotel. Other than being uncomfortable (I still had my crotch-cage on) and feeling *used*, I felt a sudden need to fight—which I was known to do rarely. Once we arrived at the hotel, we ascended many staircases and I demanded to be set free. Shane, shed of his alter ego, was a bit less severe, yet he seemed uninterested in me.

"Arms up," he said.

I lifted my hands to mouth level. Shane unlocked the cuffs and removed them. He then had me sit, in order to remove the cock-cage. My despair surfaced as rage. I wanted to scream for something but he muted my grief with his firm lips planted on mine. He then stepped back, lifted the cuffs to me and said, "I am now *thine*."

I cuffed him over his head, laid him on his belly and savored the reward of all my labor—his hairy ass. I returned his punishment through the hardness and hunger of my profound, almost spiritual, need. All the rage of my ancestors surfaced to feed my desire and the occupation of his ass—ghosts in my head shouted for freedom and drove me forward. My primordial demons feasted in the carnal celebration—they danced through fire—as I scaled the rungs of overload and came— *¡puñeta!*— with his rock-hard, mural-rich biceps in my hands, my nose pressed into the sweaty patch of bristle by his ears. I rolled off of him. My mouth split open as if I'd just died and a tide of sanity rushed over me.

When it passed, Shane asked me, "So what'd you think?"

"That I have the coolest fucking boyfriend in the universe."

Then we slept divinely, entwined like lazy vines.

COME TO LIGHT

Rhidian Brenig Jones

In the months after Stéphane, I only fucked
strangers. Pickups, chance encounters, profes-
sionals when my luck was out and my balls
were blue. One exception: when I was in
Paris, there was a cop, a thickset blond with
sultry eyes and an ass like a tourniquet. I did
him more than once—once too often. I was
picking up signs, like he wanted some kind of
connection. Sometimes, memories blindsid-
ed me and I couldn't come in him. I fucked
him even after the lube dried, which I guess he
liked, not that I gave a shit. I'd pull out and if
I was in the mood, I'd grope around some, feel
his ring strain around my wrist, but mostly I
got my face in, sucked deep into membrane
until his rising cries and savage orgasm trig-
gered me.

Cock and ass, sweat and jizz: all the connection I was looking for.

He'd called off dinner at the last moment, some situation at Beaubourg. I hung around in the restaurant, pissed and horny, and thought about calling Edouard; he's a charmless prick and expensive, but he gives fabulous head. Or a bar, maybe a club. Maybe not. The last guy who hit on me, an angel-faced Euroboy clone, twisted around midfuck, told me he loved me, then begged me to squat, take a dump on his dick.

One of the waiters called out, "*Il se fait tard, m'sieu. Il faut fermer.*"

I gave him a look. "Coupla minutes."

The window had misted up and I wiped it with my sleeve. The snow that had threatened all day had finally started and the cobblestones were whitening. The last time but one I was with Stéphane we'd been here, in Montmartre. The scene rewound and I let it play. You do it often enough, it loses its charge.

He grips my arm as he counts down, figuring I'll cheat. Rocketing up the steps, two by two, I grab at nothing as he whoops, swerves, beats me to the top. Ashen with cold in the bright December afternoon, we shiver at a sidewalk café and diss the artists in the square; such severe critics. He blows on his cup and turns his glasses to me, his eyes dancing as the steam clears the lenses. I grin and he slips his hand into my pocket, stealing warmth. His chilled fingers trace a message on my palm that makes me shift on the rickety seat, cross my legs. He murmurs against my cheek and coffee is bitter on his breath. Later, when I'm inside him, I give him the heat of my body. I move in him, moan with him, cradle him with my love. I watch his lovely face crease as his semen spurts for me. "Je t'aime, David."

Lying cunt.

The jangle of the doorbell made me jump. A tall guy came in, brushing snow from his coat, and the waiters circled him, gesticulating and bitching. He played with his keys and shot a glance in my direction. I dug around for my wallet, stopped when I saw him approach.

He smiled as he hooked out a chair. *"Vous permettez?"*

"They're about to close," I said. Enough with the frigging French.

"Ah, they will wait. It is my restaurant, this. Lucien Seignier."

"David Dos Passos."

I checked him out as he unwound his scarf. Older than me, midthirties. Dark hair, early gray above his ears. An edgy, sculpted face softened by a beautifully cut mouth. The black cashmere muffled his body but I got a sense of slenderness, fine bones. His cool hazel eyes rapidly assessed me, liked what they saw, and my dick tightened.

He sat back. "So, David, have you enjoyed your meal?"

For a second, I couldn't recollect what I'd eaten. "The duck. It was fine."

"Bien. You are having a holiday in Paris?"

"I work in La Défense."

"Yes? And what is your work?"

I should have gotten a laminated card. Essential biographical data: *Six-one, one-ninety. Black, blue. Eight inches, cut. Takes it up the ass for the right guy.* I realized I was frowning and made an effort. The man wanted to flirt a little first, where was the harm? It wasn't like I had anything better to do.

"I'm a banker," I said. "I'm based in London, come over two, three times a month."

"And what does a banker like to do in Paris when he is not...banking?"

"If I'm not doing it, I'm thinking about it."

Fine laughter lines bracketed his sexy mouth. His teeth were square and very white. One incisor jutted slightly. If I kissed, I'd lick it, run my tongue along the gum line, right to the back. But I didn't kiss tricks.

"*Bien sûr*, one must have some recreation." He picked up the wine bottle and studied the label, scratched delicately at a loose edge. His fingers were long and lightly tan and I could feel them splayed on my butt, one squirming inside, working its magic.

"Where do you stay?"

"La Boussole, it's off the rue de Poitou."

"I know this hotel, I live in Le Marais." He hesitated, then set the bottle down, dismissing it. "This is a fair wine but I have others, some fine vintages. But not here." He looked directly at me and I knew that his dick was as stiff as mine. "If you have no plans, perhaps you will care to try some?"

I didn't go home with them, either. You're in their place, their shit all around. You're all fucked out, the guy's legs are heavy on your shins and you're relaxed, a little sleepy. He talks and you turn your head on the pillow, study his profile and you think, *nice guy*. He takes your cock in his mouth again and you get so fucking hard and now it's kind of better because you like him. You see the man beyond the cock and you like him.

"David?"

I wanted to do him right there on the table, the linen cloth screwing in his fists, pain bending his spine as I split his hot French ass. The cute waiter, the young Algerian, watching from the doorway, fingering his prick, climaxing along with *Monsieur.*

"David, it is late. I think we must leave now, allow these good men to go home to their wives."

Maybe I was startled into it. Maybe the rush of blood to my dick had shut down the *Look before you leap, asshole!* center of my brain. Shit, there could have been an unusual conjunction of the fucking planets. The alarms were wailing in my head but I found myself nodding.

A brief smile tugged at the corner of his mouth. "Yes, I think you are a man who appreciates fine wine. *Alors, on va.*"

It was warm in the Lexus. He drove skillfully, hands tapping the wheel, impatient at red lights. He said something about plans to visit the Sonoma vineyards and I tuned out, peered through the windshield, not that there was anyone worth looking at. The Marais had emptied fast, even the hustlers and street vendors defeated by the swirling snow.

"Hey, Anglais!" The kid sidesteps, blocks me, flashes a grin. "Ten euros only, two for fifteen. Buy for your pretty girlfriend, yes? Your wife, also?" He waggles the gloves at me and winks. "Warm their hands."

They're kind of sweet in a cheesy way, a little elf hat atop each finger. I get an idea. I buy a pair and call in at Lafayette, pick up his favorite apricot truffles and some glittery paper. Back at the hotel, I intend to stuff the gloves with the candy but I'm so hard. I unzip, get it out. The wool is rough on my glans, stray fibers stick to the wet. I wrap the glove around my shaft, let my knees fall wide. The sensation is dulled and it's what I want. I want to masturbate for hours, forever, thinking of him. I stroke the glove back and forth over my balls, touch it to my anus, whisper his name. I visualize him, how we'll be. His gorgeous penis, rigid and glistening, sliding out. I'll be dilated from our lovemaking and he'll tilt his head as he holds me open, so he can see. The picture is suddenly in sharp focus: the way we'll share the chocolates, how he'll take them from me.

"David, *on est arrivé.*"

I glanced at the hand on my thigh. I wondered again whether Stéphane had ever opened my gift.

If my mind hadn't been on other things, I might have been impressed. Blond wood and crystal, charcoal leather sofas, the only color a vivid Heriz rug that had to be kosher: you live in the Marais, you don't do fake. I listened to him chink bottles and gave my dick a reassuring squeeze; I was headed for one staggering fuck.

He came into the room and waved two glasses at a stack of hardbacks on a low table. "You see, I try to improve my English. You like English writers?"

Chablis; a Grand Cru. I held a delicious mouthful and slid my eyes over his small, curved ass, savoring the anticipation as much as the wine. "Some," I said. "Depends."

"This one I like, she—"

I took the drinks and put them on the table. "What do you say we skip the book report?"

He smiled uncertainly, not following. I grabbed his hand and held it against my cock: universal language. "You like this?"

He liked it all right. His arm snaked around my neck and he pulled me in for a kiss. Smoothly, I lifted my jaw so he'd miss my mouth. He bit at my throat, sucking at stubble as he struggled one-handed with his zipper, couldn't get it down over the bulge. I did it for him and watched his eyes hood as I made a production of unbuttoning my own fly. I threaded my hand through damp cotton, making him flinch as I grazed a ticklish spot. His hard-on was oozing and so flinty I was scared I'd snap the thing off at the root. It lay dense and engorged, little zings of lust lifting it off my palm. I stroked a fingertip along a vein and eased the skin back to expose a succulent head, slick and pre-lubed. Frenchmen, Brits—fuck, I am so into uncut dicks. I jacked him a little and my cock clenched, angling up like it was magnetized to my belly. I groaned as he gripped it and nosed it to his own, slit to slit, in a slimy kiss.

"Oh, yeah." I steadied myself against his shoulders and looked down, watched him do it. The feel of his silky foreskin wrapping my head was so hot, so fucking erotic, my vision blurred. He was trembling and I was so turned on I almost missed what he was hissing in my ear. Almost.

"You are beautiful, *Américain*. Many men must tell you this. But...perhaps there is one, a certain man? You have a lover, David? When he does these things with you, when you are fucking, he tells you that you are beautiful? Tell me what he says."

My stomach lurched. A sick feeling washed through me and my scalp crawled.

Je t'aime, chéri. I love you.

"David?" He frowned and gently rubbed my cheek. I could smell my balls on him and the rich gaminess of our cocks.

I peeled his hand away. "I'm sorry," I said.

The flush of arousal on his face intensified, turned brick red. He gave a little laugh, then stared in disbelief as I stuffed my dying boner back into my jeans.

"I'm sorry," I said again.

"*Jésus*," he muttered.

"I mean it, man, it has nothing to do with you."

He instantly recovered his poise but his mouth was a thin, deadly line as he yanked his zipper up. "You say so? I believe it has much to do with me."

"Not true. Listen—"

"No." He crossed his arms on his chest and looked at me, his eyes narrowing as he tried to figure out how the fuck he'd gotten landed with this prick-teasing asshole. He set his jaw. "It is best if you leave."

The dim feelings of guilt I had drained away to be replaced by a sudden, livid anger. I took a step, got right in his face. "I'll be happy to, you self-righteous prick." He held his ground, didn't flicker a muscle as he stared me out. "Fuck this shit," I said softly. "Fuck it and fuck you."

My jacket had fallen off the couch. One sleeve was inside out and my hands shook as I pulled it free.

"*Américain.*"

Behind him, clots of snow as big as dimes patterned the windowpane. I thought of the walk ahead of me and flipped the collar up around my ears.

"David, we have misunderstood, there is no need for you to go." I looked at him and he shrugged ruefully. "Come," he coaxed. "You have not drunk your wine."

The air blew out of my lungs. Jesus Christ.

He sat alongside me on the sofa, nursing his glass. "I spoke of what should be private. I am sorry, I did not mean to offend you."

"Forget it."

He swirled the wine and downed it in a gulp, grimacing. I could see he was working up to something and though I was in no mood for True Confessions, I figured maybe I owed him. He hadn't meant anything by it, the guy didn't know fuck.

"Sometimes," he said, "sometimes I am with someone. I am with a man and I like to think of him with another. Two beautiful men, you understand? These two, they make love and in their passion they say things. I like to think of this. For sure, it is a foolishness, *une bêtise*. But you are beautiful, David, and to think of you with another...excites me."

Foolishness. Sweet Christ, I knew foolish. I gripped the back of my neck and stared at the rug. The colors kaleidoscoped between my feet and I shut my eyes against the growing pressure in my skull.

"He said a lot of things," I said distantly.

"Who?"

I swallowed, worked some saliva into my mouth. "I loved him, man. I loved him and he broke my fucking heart. "

I'm crossing the road to his apartment when I see his motorcycle is parked in the alley. He's gotten here before me; he must have cut a class again, little fuck. I've planned to let myself in, hide the gloves so we can play that kids' game, me calling out "hot" and "cold" until he finds them. Beyond absurd, sure, but when you're in love you do these things. You love a guy, it's not all about fucking, and with Stéphane it's not even about fucking anymore.

I hang over the rail. Below me, the basement window is dark. Chances are he'll be sprawled on the couch, plugged into his iPod. Or asleep. I want him to be asleep. It'll be almost as good, kissing my lover awake.

I insert my key and curse as the lock clicks. Two steps into the kitchen and I pause. My heart is thudding and I take shallow breaths through my mouth. I keep my eyes fixed on the crack of light framing the living room door. I'm almost there when I hear it. I cock my head, unsure. The sound comes again, clear now, unmistakable and runnels of ice water trickle through my bowels.

I'm so silent, so careful as I push the door wide.

Stéphane's body arched and straining, his face a rictus of ecstasy as the dark head moves at his groin. The guy's fingers kneading his ass, fondling the split then sinking home. Stéphane's cry, lost in the delirious rocking of his penis in and out of the desperate mouth.

Two faces turning, astonished. His arms dropping to gather the slim shoulders close, an instinctive, protecting gesture. His flat, unwavering stare, considering...calculating. My paralysis shattering as he pulls the guy to his feet and deliberately, lovingly, kisses his mouth.

I brought my hand away from my face and wiped it on my jeans. "It was Olivier," I said. "Olivier. His brother."

I surfaced to darkness, confused and disoriented. Sudden recall, my fucking *stellar* performance, crying in Lucien's arms like a retard, jolted me fully awake. I moaned inwardly, just about managed not to curl into a mortified ball and gnaw my knuckles. I lifted the duvet and sat up gingerly. He didn't move. I'd dropped my clothes in the bathroom: *grab them, get the hell out.* But first, Christ, I needed to pee.

I shook the last drops off and ran my tongue over my teeth. My mouth felt like it was lined with suede. I scooped up some water and hunted through bottles, Creed and Acqua Di Parma, until I found some Listerine. I swished a mouthful and looked around. My clothes had been neatly piled on a hamper.

Lucien…he'd been kind, listening somberly, not speaking. When it was over, he'd said I should stay "to rest, that is all, sleep if you are able." I dropped a skein of blue spit into the john and screwed the cap thoughtfully back on the bottle, tilting my chin to the mirror: still stunning. Lucien was a good guy. He was also hot and hung and naked in the bed behind me.

He'd turned onto his back, one long leg outside the covers. The light from the bathroom fell on his pale instep; the hairy, elongated diamond of his calf; the striated thigh muscles. His luscious cock was flopped soft on languid balls. I touched his toes and he opened his eyes.

"Hey," I said.

He stretched and yawned, folded his arms behind his head. The black whorls in his pits almost bridged the mat on his chest. "You are feeling better?"

"I'm feeling a whole lot better."

He dropped his eyes. "So I see."

He watched me watch his prick swell, move in jerks like the hand of a clock counting off the seconds to midnight. Sexual tension hummed between us, primal, intensely male and I thought, *There's nothing as good as this moment.* Two men, eyes locked. Cocks achingly erect, sensitive assholes beginning to stir, to loosen up just a little bit. Thundering hearts. Hungry mouths.

"So," he murmured.

"So?"

"*Encule-moi.*"

When I was fifteen, a kid in my math class told me that if you rammed hard enough into a guy, he'd come through his mouth. Seeing Lucien spread his legs for me got me so worked up I reckoned I could do it. I eased his thighs farther apart and ran my hands along the inner sides to the V of his groin. Up close, the hair in his crack brushing my lips, I caught his gut-clenching body scent: sac skin, moist perineum, the divine odor of ass.

"Oh, I'll fuck you, man." I sucked my finger, zigzagged the seam of his scrotum, and his dick flexed, balls lifting. His hole was a pink starburst, soft and yielding. I wet my finger again and that sound broke in his throat, the sound a man only hears when he's penetrating another guy, pushing high into his rectum. Low grunts of pleasure from him, from me, when I touched his prostate. I swept my finger in slow, caressing arcs and took his cock into my mouth, sucked hard until he dipped over the root of my tongue and I couldn't suck any more. I held him in my throat but I wanted him in my ass, deep inside, moving, giving me what I was about to give him. I lifted my head and slithered my finger out and curled his stickiness into my palm. "Lucien, you want me to, I'll fuck you till you bleed."

"Kiss me first."

A warm, iron ball fell tumbling inside of me and thudded to rest at the base of my dick. I stretched out on his body and took my weight on my elbows. He held my head as I nuzzled through hair, fine-spun in his armpit, a rough pelt on his chest. Searching with lips and fingertips, I found his nipples, electric, hardwired to his prick. I suckled like they were leaking sperm, his quivering thighs and fitful gasps telling me what it was doing for him. Too much. His hips came up and he began to buck, pistoning his shaft through my fist in short, staccato jabs. I gave his swollen tits a last, lingering bite and slowly relaxed my grip.

His eyes widened and he fumbled for my hand, wrestled it back to his cock. "*Finish it!*" I shook my head and he sank back to the pillow and covered his face with his arm. Although I barely touched his skin, I could feel he was losing his erection; I'd pushed him too far.

I gripped his jaw and forced him to look at me. I saw the beginnings of real hatred there, sparking in the dark, expanded pupils, but I held his gaze and something passed between us, the briefest exchange. "*Je vais t'enculer*, Lucien. I'm gonna fuck it out of you, man, fuck it *all out*." I slipped my tongue between his teeth and flicked it against his palate. The feel of soft lips yawning open, the prickling scrape of stubble, made me crazy. I kissed him clumsily, like an unpracticed teen, in a fury of clashing teeth and stabbing tongues, grinding his mouth until I had to break away or suffocate. He smiled and gave me a moment to siphon in some air, then cupped my face and guided me into a slow and tender kiss and the erotic intimacy of it turned the bones of my skull to sweet liquid.

It's part of it for me, the preparation. Rolling the condom down the length of my supersensitized cock. Keeping my eyes on the guy. Watching him bring his knees up, hold them spread on his chest. Or crouch on all fours, like Lucien did, his chin tucked into his shoulder. So ready. I propped the lube against his calf and spread his cheeks, felt the solid pelvic frame under my thumbs. I licked the hairs away, pasting them to his skin, and worked the tip of my tongue into the coppery tang of his ass, groaning when the thick ring yielded the delicacy of his rectum. I tongue-fucked him until my jawbone ached and his crack was a sopping mess of saliva and seeping ass slime, but he needed more than spit to cushion the burn. And Christ, he was going to burn. I squirted coils of gel and worked them up him, caressed the translucent glop over his sliding bag of balls and checked the stiff jut between his thighs. Fuck, yeah. He tensed as I centered, nudging for the right angle. "Okay?" He nodded and I stroked along the dip of his spine and pressed down on the blade of bone at the apex of his crack.

He yelped as I thrust, quick pain opening his ass to take my glans. The monstrous pleasure popped bright sweat on my body but I held still, waiting for the inner resistance to give. Leaning to one side, I could see his face, suffused with color, lips drawn back in a gasping snarl. So fucking beautiful. He exhaled and bore down and I was in. I'd gone beyond any thought of hurting him; I only held still, gritting my teeth, because if I'd moved I'd have shot. And I wanted to give this guy, this agonized male animal shuddering under me, the kind of fuck you read about in stroke stories.

He hung his head. A sheen of sweat oiled his skin and when I kissed his back, I felt tremors deep in the corded muscle. He reached behind, fingertips patting, searching the rim of rubber jammed against his ass. I pulled out an inch then gave it to him hard. Circling my hips in a slow, ecstatic grind, I hooked my forearms under his shoulders, swung him upright and sat back on my heels. His body jackknifed with pain and I held him, supported him, kissing the soft hair at the nape of his neck. Under my palm, inside his body, my iron-clenched fist of cock strained to his colon.

"Okay?"

"Yes."

"Sure?"

"Yes."

I wrapped his fingers around his prick. "Then do it. Get it hard."

I leaned back and watched his lean flanks hollow. Such a small ass, taut cheeks exactly fitting my hands. But the asshole enormous. Rising and falling. Taking it, loving the fullness, the stretch, the singularity of pleasure that only a stiff prick can give a guy. I felt the first, exquisite spasms ripple his gut as he moaned and stroked and I reached around and found it rigid as mine again, a stand of dickflesh rearing from his groin. Gripping his waist, I rose with him and tipped him forward and the assy stink of sex filled my nostrils. The condom was halfway up, smeared with clear mucus, and for one heart-stopping moment I thought, *Go ahead, slip it off.* I stared at the raw, red gape slowly infolding. *Slip it off.*

He grunted and arched like a cat as I fed the sodden latex back up his ass. His shoulders gathered and he pushed back in a powerful counterpoint to my driving prick. In, in, slow out and thudding in, my balls swinging with each slapping thrust, I clutched his hips, hammering him, fucking him, oh Jesus, fucking his sweet ass. A bead of sweat rolled down my temple and I raised my face to the homo gods; sent out a silent, screaming prayer for control. If the bastards were watching, they paid me no heed; my rhythm began to falter as his seething intestine kissed hot friction along every nerve in my dick. *Come on, come on, come on...* He was braced on one arm, his left hand under, doing it so slowly. He moaned as I took over, each rapid jerk, each thrust in and out of his ass edging us nearer, nearer. He came with no warning, jetting through my fingers in hard, explosive gouts; semen flying, spattering his chest with a necklace of pearls. I felt the aftershocks of climax tighten his ring and it was enough. I convulsed and cried out his name and lifted into the nuclear light of orgasm and everything became white, all white.

"Oh, man." I licked my lips. Sex always makes me thirsty as hell but I couldn't have moved if someone had leveled a shotgun at me.

Up on one elbow, Lucien grinned and began to toy lazily with my tits. I covered his hand and interlaced our fingers and it felt nice, holding him like that. I closed my eyes again and let myself drift.

He ruffled his mouth in my hair. "Was it good for you?"

I turned on my side and burrowed into his neck where the sweaty carotid beat. I drew up a sliver of skin and sucked it against my teeth. "What do you think?" I said.

"I think that it was. It was good for me, also." He pulled me closer and draped my leg over his hip. Sperm had dried on my cock so he lubed his fingers with the slick from his ass and massaged it in, deftly working the softness out. I squeezed his hard-on as he palmed my slit and did something behind my balls that made me moan like a bitch.

"God, yes, there…"

"And this time it will be better." He was half-smiling and more than the subtle, expert wank, it was the look in his eyes that transformed my shaft to rock.

"Lucien," I said, "you're gonna have to help me out here. How the fuck could it be better?"

"Yes, better. This time I will fuck you and when I make you come, it will be my name you cry, not Stéphane's. Mine."

SEX HEAD

Tim Miller

(Tim does a crazy shirt-and-clothespin dance while the tape plays and he strips naked.)

Oh. Oh. Oh. Oh.

(Tim pins clothespins all over his body. Especially strong ones on his nipples and balls. Tape fades as he begins to speak full sentences.)

Oh that feels nice. His kisses so sweet.

Those kisses so wet. Well, they're not really that wet, not in the big scheme of wetness. I just met him. I pull that READ MY LIPS shirt over my head. Do I know where his mouth has been? Well, does he know where my mouth has been? I can't be bothered worrying about saliva anyhow. I can't live in a world where we can't kiss. Does he feel me hold back? No, I think it's okay. He knows I'm a little nervous, I think.

Hey, now he's sucking my dick! Ooh, that's nice. He can do that thing way at the back of his throat that always makes me gag when I try it. Wait, if he's sucking my dick, does that mean I have to suck his? Do Unto Others as They Would Do Unto You! No, I'm an adult. I took that workshop about boundary drawing. I can say yes and no in my life. Well, maybe I'll just lick his balls for a while. That would be a friendly gesture. Well, maybe up the shaft for a bit. It couldn't hurt to just lap across the head of his dick once or twice. Maybe wrap my lips around it for a plunge up and down. Not for too long though, I don't want to have an anxiety attack tomorrow.

Gotta stay safe! Gotta stay safe!

Oooh, like in a bad Las Vegas magic act, his asshole suddenly appears at the end of my finger. The skin feels so nice, the hair there so soft.

Where's the condom? Where's the lube?

Well, one thing's for sure, if we're gonna fuck, I'm gonna be the one that fucks him. I'm negative so I'm gonna be total insta-top right? I'll just feel more comfortable then. If I let him fuck me I might have to sneak out of bed in the middle of the night and find the condom full of his cum and take it into the bathroom and fill it with water just to make sure that it didn't have a leak. I'd rather fuck him anyway. I've really gotten more into my top energy lately. It's really who I am, my deepest self, right? Ya know, now that I'm in my late thirties it's where I feel my sex pull goes most naturally. Looking at all those spread assholes in the beaver shots in *Freshman* has helped too. Yeah, all I want to do is fuck that butt! But what if I start seeing this guy regular and sometimes it's been a long day and I'm tired and I just don't have the yang savings account to smack that butt and lift those legs and huff and puff and blow my load up his pussy-boy man-cunt hot hole of my desire? What will I do then? Be in the moment.

One finger. Two finger. Three finger. Four. (It's like a song on "Barney.") This is the way we open the door. Wait, since I'm pretty mostly probably sure that I'm still negative, maybe I can fuck him without a rubber just for a while. Wow, that'd feel nice. I would feel so bad, so naughty. I should be punished. I'm such a bad boy.

Gotta stay safe! Gotta stay safe!

But what about that big *Wuthering Heights* mansion inside me that wants to put my cum in my lovers' mouths and assholes? I want to get my boyfriend Alistair pregnant. Make a baby that will lead us queer people to freedom. I can't believe I thought that. What about that part of me that wants to eat up that cum and stuff it up my butt?

Tim! You just met this guy, put on a condom and shut up!

My cock is slipping into his asshole. That feels so nice. Hey, my brain is quieting down! I'm actually in the experience of fucking another man! I'm starting to feel pretty good about myself. I think I'm a pretty great guy. I'm proud of myself finding this sex with another man. I know if my Mom were here, she would be proud of me too.

My Mom appears inside of my head with gobs of left-over Tuna Helper dripping through her fingers. "Aren't you ashamed of yourself, you dirty faggot son o' mine that will never give me grandchildren?"

Oh god, I'm losing my hard-on! Quick, think of smooth-skinned eighteen-year-old boys in wet underwear splashing in the fountains of Trafalgar Square in London.

Ashamed, Mom? No, not for this. I'm ashamed it's so hard for me to cry. I'm ashamed I shouted at that checkout person at SavOn's when I bought all these clothespins! I'm ashamed I sometimes torture the men I love. But I'm not ashamed that I like assfucking. Mom, I'm pretty busy so would you please get out of my head?

We turn the fuck upside down. I see his chest and body, his face telling me that he likes being here. His dick is getting really big and red. Every second, it looks more like Bill Clinton's face when he's jogging. Does he want me to cum in him, inside the condom? I'm getting close. Maybe I should pull out. Should I ask him? I'll just tell him. Then the ball is in his court. "I'm gonna cum!"

I'm gonna cum with bells and buzzers.

I'm gonna cum with my long curly hair.

I gonna cum with a fresh-baked pie in my hand.

I'm gonna cum with gratitude for your long legs.

I'm gonna cum with desire for the future.

I'm gonna cum with the memory of us in Fourth Grade.

I'm gonna cum with my eyes open.

I'm gonna cum with love for our bodies.

I'm gonna cum with my fear of death.

I'm gonna cum and I'm not gonna go a minute later.

I'm gonna cum...

I'm gonna cum...

I'm gonna cum...

I'm gonna cum...

I'm gonna cum...

I'm gonna cum...

THE BEST SEX BETWEEN THEM

Andy Quan

They know that they shouldn't. But the things that we know don't always help us.

"Would this be all right?" Geoffrey looks at Max searchingly.

"It's up to you." Max's expression is neither happy nor sad.

"Why is it always up to me?"

They step toward each other, not without hesitation, and kiss.

Sex had never been great between Geoffrey and Max. Their physical attraction to each other had been but it didn't seem to translate to the right chemistry. Geoffrey may have been in his forties but his body was boyish and thin with soft skin and barely a hair on his torso. For Max, it was a perfect combination of the sex appeal of wisdom and a fantasy of a young university student.

Max, on the other hand, was thick: solid neck and shoulders, a jutting chest covered with salt-and-pepper hair, and barrel-shaped thighs.

"You make my throat dry," Geoffrey told Max the first time they had sex. He was often given over to extravagant statements; he was an ad man who wanted to write novels.

The words didn't make sense to Max but the context did. Kissing was good. In fact, it was excellent: the shape of their mouths a perfect match; they would take turns naturally, licking the outside gums of the other, sucking on the other's tongue, nibbling the other's bottom lip. They lost themselves in that motion.

But the first weeks, unusually, Max couldn't come. He couldn't explain why, but he liked Geoffrey so much that it made him nervous. It short-circuited the simple order of being aroused, sexual play, and a burst of semen from the tip of one's cock.

"You don't mind, do you?" asked Max and Geoffrey admitted that if this is the way sex was going to be between them, it might be a problem.

"I like some sort of equality. It's not just about me wanting you to come. It's that I think you'll be more satisfied if you've had an orgasm too."

"But I don't mind."

Max was telling the truth but Geoffrey was unconvinced.

Geoffrey pulls up Max's rugby shirt and balances it up onto the shelf of Max's chest while he takes a great mouthful of the body that is revealed. He licks and softly bites Max's pectoral muscles, these broad round shapes. If they were vessels, they would be made of metal, thick-walled, and unable to be easily lifted when filled with water. A great chest has always been an obsession of Geoffrey's. Will he ever again find one as beautiful as this: one you can grab onto, that makes you think of strength, and makes your cock stand out sharp as a salute? They stay like that for a time before Max stretches up to lift off his shirt completely, then reaches down and eases Geoffrey out of his. It's already unbuttoned so Max eases Geoffrey's arms back, pushes gently at the fabric of the business shirt, and it wrinkles down onto the floor, Geoffrey's mouth never having lost contact with Max's chest.

The problem of orgasm (or lack of one) didn't last but instead changed into something else. It was Geoffrey this time, and at first he thought it was mental. It was the first time that his combination of antiretroviral therapy was failing and though his doctor advised him not to over-worry, he found it an impossible state, like failing to clear your mind when meditating because you are thinking the whole time about clearing your mind. So Geoffrey thought it was stress that was causing a pronounced lack of sexual drive. But after weeks, when the doctor assured him that the new medication regimen was working, he wondered if the dip in his libido could be due to his new meds.

He knew that Max was frustrated and he knew that only months into a new relationship was not a good time to draw away from sex. But he couldn't seem to do anything about it. He and Max would masturbate together; they would kiss too. But the level and intensity of lovemaking was underwhelming.

When they came back—desire, energy—the problems were

resolved only for a time. Each of them was like a singer who didn't have time to warm his vocal chords properly before a performance. He sings his way through stumblingly but the orchestra plays its final notes before he can find his way. They were never in synch.

"Have you talked about it?"

Geoffrey was seeing a counselor. He'd never done it before but he'd worried about things not working with Max. He didn't want to quit therapy unless he knew he'd put in a good effort. He was too old to give up too easily and a relationship that had only lasted a year seemed trivial. Plus he couldn't be certain that the problem wasn't something deep-seated and invisible to him but an issue that came from him rather than being mutual.

"Well, what would you like him to do? Really. Is there some situation that you can describe, some way that you would like him to be when you're having sex?"

He liked this counselor. He liked the questions that poked and prodded and made him think and talk or come to sudden revelations like this one:

"I'd like him to take charge. I'd like him to throw me onto the bed and make love to me instead of me making love to him." Geoffrey thought about big, strong Max: the odd juxtaposition of his size, and his gentle disposition. Was he hoping for something that Max just couldn't give?

Max has closed his eyes. Geoffrey is still working on his chest. It's a long foreplay before they'll get to crotch level. Geoffrey treats it as a separate sexual act, as if sexual orientations were divided into a much wider spectrum than homo, hetero and bi and he's discovered that there are only certain men with chests he can make love to. It helps when they are broad (just like it helps, frankly, to have a large penis) and it also depends on the shape and size of the nipples. Small and flat doesn't really work; the mouth glides over them, there's nothing to bite, there's little to differentiate them from the surrounding skin. What works is jutting. What works is fleshy. Of course, Geoffrey has also met men who have the perfect chests for worship but aren't interested in participating, being focused on other body parts, other motions, or being the active partner. With Max, Geoffrey's pretty much found nirvana. He can make patterns of his soft bite marks on Max's chest, the hairs of the chest brushing over Geoffrey's lips like a comb. He can suckle for long minutes the round coins of flesh with small fingertips pointing out of them, protrusions just large enough to nibble, to inhale. He licks and nips at them until these parts of Max's chest have turned the pink of roses.

It's a blow job of a different type but has a similar effect on Max, a direct pleasure circuit between what is happening on the surface of his pectoral muscles and the tip of his penis, out of which precum is forming, enough to coat its head but not enough to actually form a drop that falls onto the floor. If Max could ask for more, he'd ask to be bitten harder, a real clamp-down. But Geoffrey seems too afraid to do it. He backs off just when things are getting good. Still, Max's cock is hard with blood. He's responding to pleasure.

Geoffrey can feel this pleasure in the grip of his hand and is excited by it. The thought comes to him (which he loses, purposely, moments later) that this may be the most magnificent chest he's ever made love to and that he may never be able to do it again.

Sex was easy, Geoffrey told himself, though the truth was that it was plentiful, but not simple. Still, it could be found in saunas and sex clubs, in cruising grounds, in the locker rooms of swimming pools and gymnasiums. But someone to fall asleep with, someone to lie beside, and someone whose arms in which you can awake—how often do you find that? Geoffrey thinks that he's found quite a lot of sex in his forty-some years. But partners have been few. *Trade-offs*, he thinks. *Everything is a trade-off.* In this case, the items are sleeping together and having good sex. If he was challenged on this, he would have to back down. They did have sex. They sometimes had good sex. Sex and sleeping together were not opposite things. In fact, they were quite complementary. So he would have been forced to clarify: in this relationship, what was important to him was waking up in Max's arms, the intimacy of shared sleep, falling asleep to his partner's breathing. Really hot fucking wasn't something that could be expected or demanded. Maybe, in the end, it wasn't even that important. At least that's what he told himself.

The precum is flowing for both of them now, Max more than Geoffrey. They've rimmed each other; then Geoffrey has inserted one, then two fingers into Max and is now feeling the smooth walls of the rectum while his other hand plays with the hair on Max's belly.

They'll return to habits soon. For Geoffrey, it will be to lie on his back, with Max kneeling over him with his balls positioned over Geoffrey's mouth. Geoffrey will suck and lick and look up at Max's great form: the most beautiful view of a man, Geoffrey thinks. If he's not careful, Geoffrey will come right then, Max's hand reaching back to jerk him off. But he'll be able to restrain himself enough to slide his body and head down after one last suck on Max's balls, a lick of his arsehole. Then he'll flip himself around and get up, push Max down onto his hands and knees and fuck him slowly while reaching around and massaging his belly, especially between his belly button and crotch, the way that Max likes and requested the first time they fucked.

They will feel delicious and comfortable that they know each other's bodies, customs, and fantasies so well.

It was Max who was frustrated with the sex. But it was Geoffrey who decided to end the relationship.

"Are you happy with this?" he'd asked angrily one morning. They'd snarked at each other for days.

"No, I'm not," replied Max.

"Then you'd better figure out what you want out of this."

But that was the problem. Max didn't know. He was in love with Geoffrey—frustrating, crazy-making, annoying Geoffrey—and that was enough. He didn't demand the future. He didn't want something out of it. The present was enough to deal with, with its imperfections and lopsidedness.

Though Geoffrey didn't exactly know what he wanted either, he knew from the weight felt across his shoulders that he didn't want this.

Geoffrey is an awkward bottom, sometimes finding it hard to relax, unable to be penetrated if a cock is too thick or too long. So he has always marveled at how open Max is, how relaxed and flexible his anus is. Not only that but his flexibility in general. Such a big man but he can lift his knees up so they touch his shoulders and then even stretch his legs out nearly straight from there.

The condoms are out. A wrapper falls away easily. Lubri-cant is pumped onto a palm and then smeared onto latex, and onto skin. Geoffrey enters Max easily in one plain motion, simpler than speech, quicker than argument. The slight fric-tion between their body parts creates heat like swallowing a mouthful of whiskey. .

He fucks him for a while in Max's favorite position, kneeling over with Geoffrey's hand on his belly. But this time, they're really going to make it last, they'll fuck as long as they can, as hard as they can—in no particular order: lying on the bed from the side, one of Max's legs lifted and resting on Geof-frey's shoulder; standing, Max's right hand balancing against the corner of a wardrobe for balance, Geoffrey behind him, his hands on each side of Max's shoulders, thrusting; Geoffrey lying on his back, Max on top facing him, leaning down oc-casionally to kiss.

Like a concerto that returns to the theme of its opening bars, they return to their first tableau: the same action and postures. Max squeezes all of the muscles inside of him, like holding in laughter. He feels his sphincter and anus constrict around Geoffrey's cock. Geoffrey gasps and moans at the same time.

It's as good as it's ever been. Why couldn't sex have been as unencumbered when they were together? Geoffrey is free of a dozen worries and a dozen insecurities—among them: Do we always have to do it the same way? Do I always have to be the top? Am I enjoying this? Worst of all but perhaps hidden, even to Geoffrey himself: if it's good, really good, does it mean that we should be together forever?

Max feels the same liberty and joy. Gone is the worry of whether Geoffrey loves him as much as he loves Geoffrey. Of whether Max is attractive enough. Or whether he is truly the ideal lover that Geoffrey wanted. He's happy, so very much so, to fall into the motion of truly great sex; that Geoffrey is not holding back; that there is force in these thin but strong arms, grabbing him and making him into an object of pleasure.

They shouldn't really be doing this in any case, this forbidden act of sleeping with one's ex, of making the messy messier, of complicating matters considerably and doing what all your friends say you shouldn't do. Breaking taboos can cause even more excitement. Not that they'll do it again—in different ways, they both know that. It makes this last time all the more sweet.

It was just a visit to pick up the last of his possessions but Geoffrey senses that he won't return. He doesn't feel sad but there's an empty, unanswered feeling, like wandering into the entryway of a run-down old home, and calling out to see if anyone is there.

With some difficulty, he opens the front door to leave Max's apartment building. His hands are each carrying a few large plastic bags, and on top of this he's balancing a small box of miscellanea. He manages to put it all into his car then frets—*there he goes again*—turning circles in his mind:

Will what they did make it harder to be...friends? Is that what they'd be? Cordial ex-boyfriends? In contact?

Yes, it will make things more difficult. But, he decides—his heart beating fast and at an erratic pace—it was worth it. Well worth it.

Max, meanwhile, doesn't think as much, or at least, he pretends not to. There are things that he's putting out of his mind already: the lead-up, the background story, the dialogue. It won't happen right away but eventually he'll be left with just memories of the physical act and the windstorm of emotions that accompanied it. Now, he remembers Geoffrey's head, the dead weight of it, on his right side on top of where his chest and stomach meet, resting on his torso after this last sex, this best sex they've ever had. He knows that it's ridiculous but honestly it feels like there's still an indentation there, as if in a down pillow after a deep, motionless sleep. It will take time to fill in again, for his body to regain form.

UNDERGROUND OPERATOR

Andrew McCarthy

Nowhere in New York City is July's inescapable heat more viscerally punishing than below ground, where the atmospheric pressure rises with the descent into the subway. The potent odor of decay and fermented urine, occasionally peppered with bleach or ammonia by maintenance staff, offers little comfort to the unfortunate traveler who is eager to be elsewhere. Worst are evening rush hours, when trains are packed with fatigued commuters, collectively worn down by the day's work and the unforgiving humidity.

Even subway sounds are assaulting: the unintelligible squawk box announcements, the high-pitched gnashing of metal wheels on curving rails, the thunderous rattle of train bodies squeezing their rectangular shapes through winding tunnels. Before a train arrives at a station with its familiar screeching, ironically signaling a relief from some of the subway's other sensory hostilities, platform inhabitants contemplate their abilities to overcome the suffering inherent with waiting for and riding the train.

Will I find a newspaper on the platform bench so I have something to read, or use to wave warm air from side to side in an attempt to cool down? Is there any water left in the bottle in my bag? Do I have a rag to wipe the sweat off of my face, or to slide under my shirt to sponge off my damp back? When the train finally comes, will I get a seat? Most importantly: will the train be air-conditioned? The answer must always be yes in order to preserve sanity.

Regardless of the journey's length, it will never be easy or luxurious. Once I'm on the train, there is no shortage of nuisances, starting with the barrage of advertisements, to which only the blind possess immunity. Portable music players, intended to shield their owners from the subway's annoying sound effects, are turned up to inappropriate volumes, creating their own unwelcome environmental disturbances. Numerous are the loud, inane conversations of callous adults who should know better than to be so tactless. As for the ever-present boisterous adolescents, they could care less about socially appropriate behavior in public spaces. Panhandlers and subway preachers transgress boundaries further than do rib-poking shoulder bags; their grief, desperation, and diatribes remind us how much we want to be home, where privacy is guaranteed.

Fulton Street train station is the busiest subway complex in lower Manhattan, linking four train lines and serving nearly three hundred thousand passengers daily. Of those four train lines, the BMT is the least busy, and boasts only one real transportation asset: the M train. Starting in Middle Village, Queens, the M makes a few stops in lower Manhattan, and then runs into southern Brooklyn, but only until about eight o'clock at night. Afterward, passengers can take the J train, which shares a portion of its route with the M, running from Queens into Manhattan. The big difference is that the J terminates one stop after Fulton Street, in the sleepy financial district. Late at night, J trains arriving at the deserted downtown Fulton Street station carry few passengers, and fewer, if any, people wait to board the train. People still wait on the platform, but not necessarily for the train.

Long after crowded subway cars are vacated by passengers who think themselves entitled to imaginary and invented private space, the intersections of public and personal intimacy are explored on the platform. And this is where my story begins.

The Brooklyn-bound #2 train I was on pulled into Fulton Street around ten o'clock. I got out and navigated through the maze of passages and staircases to the downtown J train. Moving slowly through the palpable heat of the quiet station, I looked around and saw no one. The platform arcs in a way that leaves its northern section obscured, and that is where I headed, hoping to find a piece. As I approached the end of the platform, a figure became visible from behind one of the many steel-beam columns that run from the floor to the ceiling of the station. As I got closer, a well-kept, stocky brother revealed himself.

I eased my stride, checking him out as I walked to the column behind the one he was leaning on. My man was in his late thirties, shorter and heavier then me—about five foot eight inches tall, weighing about one hundred seventy pounds— light-brown-skinned, with a mustache and shaved head. Dark blue jeans wrapped tightly around his hefty thighs, and a thin, sky-blue basketball tank top hung from his shoulders, draped over his burly torso. Large white vinyl letters spelled out Rim Rokka. His arms were big, and any muscular definition was subtle. This man was undeniably hot.

Positioned opposite him, my back against the metal girder, I reached my right hand down to grab my crotch while my left hand rubbed my chest through my fitted tank top. The resonant buzz of the fluorescent lights above characterized the tense contemplation that filled the next few seconds before either of us made a move. Finally, his thick fingers pulled at the bulge in his jeans. This single gesture answered my greeting with affirmation, and I stepped nearer.

Standing in front of him now, both of us still pawing at our dicks, I ran my free hand across his meaty chest, excited by the firmness and impressive size of his broad pecs. He narrowed his eyes and opened his mouth, sighing as I brushed his stiffening nipples. My hand found its way below his shirt, sliding up his smooth hard belly to his chest, where my fingers rolled his right nipple, then his left. Leaning into him, grinding my waist into his, my eyes caught the first sight of his naked upper body as he raised his shirt over his head to lay it across the back of his neck, signaling his commitment to this encounter. His robust muscular build, covered in a thick layer of skin, seemed natural; definitely sexier than a gym-manufactured sculpture.

I made sure that there was no one else around by craning my neck to look past the column we were hiding behind. My man's hand gently pulled me back, drawing my head lower to his chest. My lips parted as they made contact and my tongue flicked across the tips of his nipples. Cradling me in his burly forearm, he guided my head back and forth as my mouth re-moistened the dried sweat that flavored his skin salty. I lifted my tank top to give him access to my nipples, which he rubbed and made firm. He then freed my growing dick from my jeans and dug out my balls with two fingers, massaging them before palming my cock. He spoke for the first time. "Damn. You got some big dick, Pa. You gonna break me off a piece of this?" His voice was as deep as his intent. Smiling, and feeling up his trade through the fabric of his jeans, I replied "Hell yeah! Let's get to work."

He squeezed as much of my dick as could fit in his hand, hardening me further. Shaking his head, his eyes locked on me as he unfastened his belt and loosened his pants. I pulled down his jeans and boxers to find his already-hard dick and balls nestled between his massive legs. He was smaller then me— about five inches long—and had a tight foreskin that pulled back from a shiny pink head. Both our dicks curved upward, but my fat head was his focus. Crouching down, my man lift-ed my low-hanging nuts to meet his lips, sucking them into his mouth one by one. His mustache crushed into the base of my dick as I bounced its head against his jaw, letting him know what was next.

Shorty repositioned himself and was kneeling before me on the filthy platform floor. He was not here to waste time, which was perfect for me, because I meant business. I pushed my crotch into his face as he sucked my balls. "Harder. Suck 'em harder," I instructed as I cupped his head in my hand, pulling his face into my groin. A cherry-flavored condom was fished from my pocket and rolled down to the base of my dick. I receded to get enough room for brandishing my trade, show-ing off the piece he was going to eat. My dick bobbed in the air before he took hold of it, pulling me closer as his mouth and eyes opened wide.

His lips and tongue ushered my cock into his wet mouth, and the intensity of the pleasure matched the density of the hot humid air. He got me harder by rotating his head from left to right as he sucked. His hand wrapped around my cock and followed his mouth up and down my piece while his tongue licked my shaft. On the way down, he'd remove his hand so that he could take all of me inside of him until his mustache blended with my pubic hair. Increasing the speed and strength with which he sucked, my man grabbed the back of my legs for leverage as he jerked back and forth. His head nodded furi-ously up and down, and I writhed on the platform, desperately trying to keep my groaning to a minimum.

Suddenly my dick popped out of the cocksucker's mouth as he coughed and spit, then climbed up off his knees. Standing in front of me, his chest lifting with heavy breathing, he panted, "Fuck me, yo." He pulled his pants down past his knees as he turned around and bent over, bracing himself on the column in front of us. Brother man stretched his arm back and pulled his left cheek out of the way, exposing his hairless hole to the air and to my throbbing cock. He was already wet and opening up, inviting me to slide in. It's a good thing I packed a bottle of lube with the condoms I was carrying, because I like to get up in a man when his ass is sloppy and juicy. After lubing my dick, I grabbed his other asscheek and closed in on his hole, pushing the knobby head of my cock inside, then plunging in until our legs smacked together.

"*Ugh!*" The words were exhaled in a rush as he arched his

back, all an involuntary response to the sensation of sudden penetration. "Yeah, Pa, I got some dick for you," I said as I pulled all the way out and rammed back into his ass. My man let go off his asscheek and reached back to pull on mine, driving me further inside him. He pushed back on me as I boned him with long steady thrusts. We kept at this rhythm, and the sound of our bodies banging together echoed off the tiled walls.

In defiance of our public setting's limitations, he began to wail loudly as I repeatedly jammed my dick into his fleshy ass. Our sexual transformation of the train platform heightened the urgency of our horny aggressions. Bending over him, I laid my chest against his broad sweaty back, and wrapped my hand over his mouth to keep him quiet. My fingers were sucked into his mouth as he grunted: "Fuck me! Fuck me!" His hand still clung to me but had slid down my leg, his fingers digging deeper into my hamstrings. Both of us pulled on each other, frenzied with lust. "Take this dick, man. Take this dick!" I demanded as my hips pounded against him. He flexed the muscles in his ass, squeezing my dick and tickling all of my nerve endings.

In his current bent-over position, and with both of us throttled by sensations, neither of us noticed that we were not alone. Walking up the platform toward us was a guy I'd seen cruising before, immediately recognizable by his dark complexion and Trinidadian flag handkerchief tying back his shoulder-length dreadlocks. I kept fucking so as not to alarm my partner.

The newcomer arrived, proceeding with a cautious pace, and stopped a few feet away to watch. He looked around thirty, slim, and roughly six feet tall. A light beard complemented his handsome angular features and conveyed a sense of appealing masculinity. He was wearing gray sweat shorts with a matching zip-up short-sleeved shirt that was embroidered in red with a simple graffiti-style crown across the chest; it was the logo for the hip-hop clothing company PNB, whose acronym had many original meanings, such as "Post No Bills" and "Proud Nubian Brothers." Tonight, it meant "Poppa Needs Bicho."

Triniman's dick was already raising the right leg of his shorts by the time his hand grabbed hold of his trade and gently shook it. I raised an eyebrow and jerked my head in my direction, inviting him to come over. As he did, the guy I was dicking down saw him and stood up to better view the dude and assess the situation. Just then, we heard the train as it screeched through the tunnel leading into the station. Quickly, hard-ons were tucked away and clothing was pulled back into place as we dispersed.

From our separate locations, we instinctively took inventory of the passengers on the passing J train, looking for uniformed cops or transit workers who might get out and investigate our reasons for loitering since we had not boarded the train. One woman with a large plastic shopping bag exited the middle of the train and left the platform, presumably to transfer to one of the other subway lines. No one got on the train, and only the three of us remained. Before the last few cars of the J snaked out of the southern end of the station, we were already positioning ourselves to resume our tryst.

The dread's bulge was still present, and both me and the guy I was fucking were eager to sexplore his package. He unzipped his shirt and its two sides parted, uncovering a hairy chest and solid, worked-out stomach. The bottom again raised his jersey, and my tank top also came up. Fingers tweaked nipples, and hands fondled growing dicks through our pants. I liberated my dick and started to pull at it. The heavyset guy unbuckled and lowered his jeans, and bent over to start sucking on the Trini's dick, which came out for the first time. His cock was fat like a cucumber and about nine inches long. A thick foreskin hung over the tip, laced by ropelike veins, as much of his body was. He started tugging at my dick while I played with his nipples. The light-skinned dude slobbered on the new cock for only half a minute before turning around to take it up his horny ass. I gave the baller a condom to put on, and they started fucking.

As Trini's dick pushed into the beckoning hole, the bottom began moaning loud enough to get us all busted. I wrapped up my piece in a mint-flavored hood and maneuvered in front of him so he could give me head. This shut him up. He reached for my leg to brace himself as he started beating his meat, and I steadied his shoulders. The blow job was messy and not as methodical as before since his concentration was on his back getting banged out. Drool leaked out of my sucker's mouth as he gasped for air. He intermittently choked on my dick as the stud plowing him forced him forward every time they crashed together.

"Fuck that ass!" I hissed to turn them on more.

"Yuh dun know," the Trini confirmed in an accent as thick as curry stew from Sunday night cook-up as he juked the man in front of him harder. Sweat began to form on the top's skin. I wanted a taste of the glistening sweat droplets in his body hair, so I arched my back over the man between us and planted my face in the Trinbagoan's bulky tits. Surrounded by coils of black hair, his nipples stiffened inside my mouth as my tongue wiggled over them one at a time. His breath blew forcefully past my ear as he fucked our bottom brother. The top's hand buried my head in his muscular chest as his momentum grew faster. The guy getting screwed was moaning in high pitches, almost crying, getting ready to cum as his body jerked powerfully. He yelped as his whole body shook with the fury of busting his nut. The spray of his gray-white cum flew everywhere, coating my lower legs and the cement floor.

Resuming normal posture, the bottom retrieved a washcloth from his back pocket and wiped off his sweat-soaked body. After his breathing normalized and he gathered himself, he smiled at us and said, "This shit was mad hot. One." Then he bounced from the scene. This left me and the man with the big bamboo. He'd taken off the condom and tossed it into the tracks, and was now playing with his long cock, rolling his foreskin back and forth on his big dickhead. His trade bowed downward and curved to the left, and was still hard. He laid his hand on my shoulder and pressured me downward to blow him. "Your time to taste de cocoa," he asserted.

Squatting in front of him, I stretched a condom over his piece while I licked the insides of his hairy thighs, passing my tongue over the many veins detailing his skin's surface. With one hand wound around the base of his shaft, I opened my mouth and wrapped my lips and tongue around his glans, sliding my mouth down as far as I could go until he hit the back of my throat. I repeated this a few times before swallowing his cock whole, gagging on its girth and length. "Mmmmm..." he groaned. I looked up at him as I brought my lips all the way to the base of his cock again. He grasped the sides of my head and started to fuck my face. The strength of his motions almost knocked me down, so I slid my hands up beneath his shorts, laying my palms on his quads to steady myself.

After a couple of minutes, my man pulled me up so we stood face-to-face. My heart was racing. In one movement, the dread cocked his head, parted his lips, and we started kissing. Our tongues braided together in a passionate electric charge. I closed my eyes and opened up to this sexy stranger, forgetting about the stifling heat, the decrepit plaster ceiling falling apart above our heads, and the dangers we flirted with tonight in the subway—and every day—for being gay. We ignored the threat of hostility, and accepted our vulnerability by creating this pleasurable intimacy behind enemy lines. Fuck the police. We were going to fuck each other.

Arms searched for flesh unvisited by touch, eager to deliver affections. His hands found my backside and I found his interest. He started to pry at the opening of my ass, and I wet his fingers with lube. Gently, he entered me with an index finger and began massaging my insides as we continued kissing. I gripped his cock and lubed it up, because he wanted to lay some pipe, and it had to fit with ease. Our tongues untangled as he pulled away to spit on his cock. "I'm gonna mash up this bamsee, boy!" he declared.

"Ya promise?" I teased.

"Fuh true."

I turned around and bent over, then backed onto his piercing fat cock. The initial pain of the penetration flashed up my spine, but soon was replaced with a flood of ecstasy. No balling in recent memory felt this good. "Yeah," he breathed heavily as he jammed himself faster into my ass. I stretched my arms back to twist his nipples between my fingers, letting go when his chest pushed into my back as he folded himself over on top of me. Then one of my hands grabbed the column that we hid behind while the other worked my dick.

He gripped my waist roughly, pounding his hips against me, and I took all of him inside of me. My nerves were more stimulated each time he forced his cock into my ass. "Damn, this dick is good. Pump that ass, Pa!" I half whispered. Brother man kissed me as he massaged my prostate with his strokes. His tongue ran up my neck and into my ear. His mouth was on my ear as he asked, "You like this cockstand, baby?"

"Hell yeah! Give me all that dick. No mercy on my ass."

The grindsman let go of my waist, and hugged me with great strength, grunting as he bucked more powerfully than before. He rushed into me faster and harder, and built up so much speed that I began biting his arm to keep from screaming out loud. My ass surely was going to ache from the beating, but the sensory overload felt so good. I tilted my pelvis upward to provide better access to my hole, and I jacked my dick. "You got some cum for me? I wanna see you shoot it." I managed to get the words out between gasps for air. My man loosened his grip on my shoulders and climbed off my back. He yanked off the condom to beat his flesh raw. My mouth instinctively found itself on his nipples, and I pumped my own cock as we both edged toward the explosion of orgasm.

"Oh!" He strained to drag the breath from the depths of his spasming frame as he busted. His brawny arms and hairy pecs tensed as he heaved forward, pressing himself into my side while he beat his dick faster and tighter. Streams of cum shot across the platform and down into the darkness of the tracks. The end of his load dribbled down his fist and into the wiry black pubic hair at the base of his thick cock, now resplendent with the iridescent liquid. I furiously jerked my dick until I came, lacing his stomach with liquid pearls that streamed down the contour of his tight abdomen.

I pinned the dread against the I-beam, our moist bodies connecting in the heat. We kissed and squeezed each other with exhilaration until the familiar smell of burned diesel fuel from a work train began to fill the air. Both of us scrambled to assemble ourselves before the train made it through the tunnel and into the station. I wiped off my hands on my chest and legs before lowering my shirt and pulling up my pants. My partner in sex crime rubbed his hands together in an attempt to dry them off before zipping up. He slapped my ass and grinned as we left the scene.

The soot-covered yellow work train winded through the station after blowing its deafening horn twice. Black exhaust clouds billowed into the air. The train was comprised of about eight cars, most of which were flatbeds that carried dozens of dumpsters. The containers were full of trash that had been collected from all of the other stations along the J line. The poignant smell of rot was overwhelming.

I asked where my man was headed, and he said he was going to Brooklyn on the #2 train. "Me too," I said with a feeling of serendipity. He facetiously asked if it was because I was coming back to his place. The answer would always be yes.

ABOUT THE AUTHORS

SHANE ALLISON, when not giving blow jobs to college boys through university bathroom glory holes, is writing stories about the college boys he has given blow jobs to through the bathroom glory holes of universities in Florida and beyond. His stories have graced the pages of *Best Black Gay Erotica, Dorm Porn 2, Ultimate Gay Erotica 2006* and *2007, Truckers, Cowboys, Hustlers, Sexiest Soles* and *Best Gay Erotica 2007*. He is the editor of *Hot Cops: Gay Erotic Stories*. Thugs, punks, nerds, married men and scarred-up, skinny white boys can drop him emails and nudey pics at starsissy42@hotmail.com.

TOM CARDAMONE is the author of the erotic fantasy novel *The Werewolves of Central Park*.

He has several projects, fiction and nonfiction, on the horizon. Read some of his short, sharp, speculative stories at his website, www.pumpkinteeth.net.

WAYNE COURTOIS is author of the novel *My Name Is Rand,* part of which appeared in *Best Gay Erotica 2005.* Two new books—a second erotic novel and a memoir—are forthcoming. He lives in Kansas City, Missouri, and can be found at www.waynecourtois.com.

ARDEN HILL is an all-around queer with an MFA in creative writing from Hollins University. His primary partner and genre is poetry, though he enjoys encounters with erotica, creative nonfiction, and the critical essay. Arden is currently a poetry editor for Breath and Shadow, an online journal of disability culture and literature. His first book of poetry is forthcoming from Side Show Press.

LEE HOUCK was born in Chattanooga, Tennessee and now lives in Queens, New York. His work includes original pieces for theater seen in Vermont, Tennessee and New York City, an essay in *From Boys to Men,* and poetry in the Magnetic Poetry Calendar. Additionally, he has created art installations for the Musee de Monoian, and has worked with Jennifer Miller's Circus Amok for ten seasons. He is at work on his second novel. The first one, *Yield,* is looking for a home. For more, go to www.leehouck.com.

RHIDIAN BRENIG JONES lives in Wales, getting overexcited by ideas for stories and by the men who inspire them.

JEFF MANN's work has appeared in many literary journals and anthologies. He has published two collections of poetry, *Bones Washed with Wine* and *On the Tongue*; a book of personal essays, *Edge*; a collection of poetry and memoir, *Loving Mountains, Loving Men*; and a volume of short fiction, *A History of Barbed Wire*. He teaches creative writing at Virginia Tech in Blacksburg, Virginia.

ANDREW McCARTHY is a multidisciplinary artist originating from New York City. He cofounded, designed, and has written for a few defunct gay publications over the last ten years, and has published a collection of poetry, *Living Beyond Deadline: Hysteria In Verse*. Forthcoming is a second volume, *Outlaw Subverses*. Visit alterarts.net for a taste of his art, including photos of Andrew in drag as Jennifuh Leathuh.

SAM J. MILLER is a community organizer. He lives in the Bronx with his partner of six years. When he's not writing or organizing poor people to fight for social justice, he's binging on silent movies and punk rock. Drop him a line at samjmiller79@yahoo.com.

TIM MILLER's solo performance work, hailed for its humor and passion, has delighted and emboldened audiences all over the world. He is the author of the books *Shirts & Skins*, *Body Blows*, and *1001 Beds*, an anthology of his performances and essays that won the 2007 Lambda Literary Award for best book in Drama. Miller is the cofounder of Performance Space 122 in NYC and Highways Performance Space in Santa Monica, CA. He can be reached at his website: http://hometown.aol.com/millertale

ANDY QUAN, author of the full-length collection of erotica, *Six Positions*, and of *Calendar Boy* (short fiction), *Slant* (poetry), and the forthcoming *Bowling Pin Fire* (also poetry), is happy to return to the *BGE* family after a few years away, during which he's added Australian on top of his North American nationalities. He's obsessed with succulents, is reviving the art of the mix tape in CD form, practices Reiki, sings songs, and occasionally updates his website, www.andyquanmusic.com.

SIMON SHEPPARD is the editor of *Homosex: Sixty Years of Gay Erotica,* and the author of *In Deep: Erotic Stories; Kinkorama: Dispatches From the Front Lines of Perversion; Sex Parties 101* and the award-winning *Hotter Than Hell and Other Stories.* His work has appeared in about two hundred fifty anthologies, including many editions of *The Best American Erotica* and many, many of *Best Gay Erotica.* He writes the syndicated column "Sex Talk," the online serial "Dirty Boys Club," and hangs out at www.simonsheppard.com.

JASON SHULTS' work has appeared online in Blithe House Quarterly and Velvet Mafia, and in several print publications, including the anthology *Fresh Men: New Voices in Gay Fiction.* He owns a bookstore in Tucson, Arizona, and is at work on a novel.

TAYLOR SILUWÉ studied creative writing at NYU and is assistant editor for *Out IN Jersey* magazine. His short stories "A Taste for Cherries" and "When Romeo Awakes" appeared in the anthologies *Tough Guys* and *Law of Desire* respectively. He can be found sounding off on his website www.TaylorSiluwe.com or in his column for *FlavaLIFE* magazine.

HOREHOUND STILLPOINT is a San Francisco waiter/writer who's been around forever. He's a story in Justin Chin's *Burden of Ashes* and he was the muse, supposedly, for Ian Philips' *Satyriasis*. His work has been widely published in anthologies such as *Poetry Slam*; *Poetry Nation*; *Out in the Castro*; *Pills, Thrills, Chills and Heartache*; *From Boys to Men*; *Porn!* and *I Do, I Don't*. Seven recent poems are collected in *Bullets & Butterflies*. He was part of the award-winning Daytrippers theater group, and had plays in the S. F. Fringe Festival in 2000 and 2001. *Reincarnation Woes*, with illustrations by KRK Ryden, is a mini-book out on Kapow! Press, but it is probably not in a bookstore anywhere near you.

CHARLIE VAZQUEZ is the slippery author of novels, novellas, screenplays, queer art essays and erotica. He is a bossy clown, a retired sex-toy clerk, and the personal assistant to diva-chanteuse Diamanda Galás, in New York City. He is actively seeking a literary agent. More info: www.firekingpress.com.

ALANA NOËL VOTH is a single mom who lives in Oregon with her ten-year-old son, one dog, two cats, and several freshwater fish. Her fiction has appeared in *Best Gay Erotica 2007* and *2004*, *Best American Erotica 2005*, *The Big Stupid Review*, and *Literary Mama*.

ABOUT THE EDITORS

Emanuel Xavier is author of the poetry collections *Pier Queen* and *Americano,* and the acclaimed novel *Christ-Like.* He is also editor of the anthology *Bullets & Butterflies: queer spoken word poetry.* He has performed throughout the country as a spoken word poet and received cultural awards for his contributions as a gay Latino artist.

Richard Labonté has edited the *Best Gay Erotica* series since 1997. He writes the occasional newsletter, *Books To Watch Out For*, and the fortnightly book review column, "Book Marks," distributed by Q Syndicate. With Lawrence Schimel, he is coeditor of *The Future is Queer* and *First Person Queer*, for Arsenal Pulp Press. He has edited *Hot Erotica*, *Country Boys*, *Best Gay Romance 2008* and *Where the Boys Are* for Cleis Press, where he is also an editor at large. He lives on Bowen Island, British Columbia, with the Pacific Ocean for a backyard, and on a farm in rural eastern Ontario, surrounded by two-hundred acres of hay fields.